SPLITSVILLE

The Lip Gloss Chronicles

SPLITSVILLE

The Lip Gloss Chronicles

SHELIA M. GOSS

www.urbanbooks.net

Urban Books
1199 Straight Path
West Babylon, NY 11704

Splitsville copyright © 2009 Shelia M. Goss

ISBN- 13: 978-1-60162-188-7
ISBN- 10: 1-60162-188-4

First Printing October 2009
Printed in the United States of America

10   9   8   7   6   5   4   3   2   1

Distributed by Kensington Publishing Corp.
Submit Wholesale Orders to:
Kensington Publishing Corp.
C/O Penguin Group (USA) Inc.
Attention: Order Processing
405 Murray Hill Parkway
East Rutherford, NJ 07073-2316
Phone: 1-800-526-0275
Fax: 1-800-227-9604

SPLITSVILLE

The Lip Gloss Chronicles

1

The D Word

"**J**asmine McNeil, you are our new Miss Teen USA," Usher announced to me and the world.
Teary-eyed, dressed in a violet floor-length evening gown, I accepted the tiara and huge bouquet of roses and walked down the runway waving at the audience and the cameras. I wasn't at a loss for words. "I would like to thank my mom and dad for believing in me. If it wasn't for their genes I wouldn't be as beautiful as I am. I would like to thank my best friends back in Dallas, Britney Franklin and Sierra Sanchez. Oh, and one other thing, I wanted to thank all the haters—look at me now." Someone was beating some drums, trying to ruin my moment. I looked around but couldn't see who because of the blinding light.

"Jasmine Charlotte, get your butt ready for school,"

my mom's voice rang from over my bed, waking me up from my dream.

I attempted to pull the covers back over my head, but she wasn't having it. Once I realized she wasn't going away, I slowly rose up out of the bed. My mom didn't let her five-foot stature stop her from laying down the law in our house. My sister and I would call her Lil' Kim behind her back when she made us mad. Her full name was Kimberly Ann McNeil and she wore the name like a badge of honor. She was proud to be the wife of the ex-NFL superstar Dion McNeil. With folded arms, she stood and watched as I got my stuff together. "Mom, I'm not a little kid. I can get dressed by myself."

She tapped her foot a few times before responding. "If you stayed off that computer, you could get up. I'm really thinking about having it taken out."

"Mom, please," I begged. "I promise I won't stay up late anymore." I avoided eye contact and made a beeline for my closet, ignoring my mom's rants.

"I'll think about it. Hurry up, because Brenda has to register for her classes today and she's dropping you off at school first."

"Mom, I thought you were dropping me off."

"Jasmine, I don't have time for your attitude. Just get ready and don't make your sister late."

I heard the door slam. I looked out my closet door

and my mom was nowhere in sight. Lately it didn't take much to set her on a verbal rampage. She and my dad fought the entire two weeks we were out on winter break. For the first time in a long time, I actually looked forward to going to school.

An hour later, I found myself rushing because Brenda wanted to annoy me by honking her horn instead of telling me she was ready to leave. She was my older sister and in college but sometimes she could act so immature. With my backpack in one hand and my favorite lip gloss, Grape Delight, in another, I rushed by my mom at the end of the stairway as she gave me the evil eye.

"What took you so long?" Brenda asked. She pulled off before I could get my seat belt on.

"You better not let Mom or Dad see you pulling off like that."

"Please. Mom and Dad got too many other problems, so I know they're not concerned about my driving."

"What do you mean?"

"Don't know if I should tell you with that type of attitude." She honked her horn at the car in front of us.

"Bren, come on. If you know something, tell me."

"Mom and Dad are thinking about getting a divorce."

"A di—" I couldn't say the word.

"Yes, a divorce. I know you've heard them. Everybody on the block probably did . . . as loud as they are." By now, we were stuck at the light on the corner of Legacy Drive and Plano Boulevard.

"They can't get a di—" Brenda's news shocked me. I couldn't even say the *d* word. My parents argued, but didn't everybody's? I didn't realize it had gotten so bad they were talking about splitting up for good. *Why was this happening to me? Why? Why? Why?*

"People get divorced all of the time."

"But not our parents. We're a family. What'll happen to us?"

Brenda dodged between cars as we neared Plano High School. "News flash, I'm grown. I'll be twenty this year and you're fourteen going on forty. I think we can take care of ourselves."

"This is not how I planned on spending my high school years."

"Grow up. This is the real world, baby."

I was late so Britney and Sierra had already left for our homeroom class by the time I made it to school. It was hard concentrating on Mrs. Johnson when my mind stayed on my parents and the bombshell Brenda dropped on me. If they were getting a divorce, why didn't they say something to me? Did they not care how their actions would affect me? Parents could be so selfish.

I wrote Britney a quick note about what Brenda told me. I signed it with a frown face instead of my normal smiley face. We exchanged a few notes back and forth. She was just as surprised as I was about my parents' situation.

"Jasmine McNeil, if I catch you or Ms. Franklin passing notes in my class one more time, you will be sent to the office. Understood?" Mrs. Johnson, my homeroom teacher, asked, as she confiscated the note I passed Britney.

"Yes," I mumbled.

"I didn't hear you."

It seemed she was set on embarrassing us. I responded louder. "Yes, ma'am."

Britney, my best friend since elementary school, acknowledged she heard her too. I wished I was at home watching something on MTV instead of listening to Mrs. Johnson go on and on about nothing. When the bell rang, I rushed out to meet Britney and Sierra in the hallway.

Britney, with her long chestnut-brown streaked hair like my favorite singer Beyoncé, and Sierra, who had a body like Jennifer Lopez but was only fourteen, were talking about Mrs. Johnson when I walked up to them.

"I can't stand her," I said, not caring who heard me.

Britney said, "This is the first day back from winter break and she's already tripping."

"I'm surprised she said anything to her favorite student," Sierra teased.

I rolled my eyes at her. "Well, I don't have time for her nonsense. I'm dealing with enough as is."

"Maybe Brenda's wrong," Sierra tried to assure me.

"Ladies, you need to get to class," the hall monitor interrupted us.

We all had different second-hour teachers so we went our separate ways. Sierra could be right. Brenda did like to exaggerate things so maybe she was wrong. There was one way to find out. I took out my cell phone and sent my mother a quick text message. She responded back that we would talk later.

Not a good sign at all. She could have said I was wrong, but she didn't. Divorce. I never thought it would affect me and now here I was facing it whether I wanted to or not.

2

Life's Remix

"Jas, I know you still want me," Dylan Johnson said as he tried to block me from my locker. Several of his friends stood nearby. One person missing from his small entourage was his cousin, Marcus.

Since he brought an audience, I decided to put on a show. I pushed his arm away. "DJ, you need to get a life and get out of mine."

"Don't be mad because I chose your friend over you."

I looked him up and down. "Don't get it twisted. You and I both know I dumped you first. Why? Because I knew you weren't worthy of all of this." I moved my hands up and down my body.

His friends laughed. I leaned against my locker with my arms folded. I didn't move until he moved. DJ said a few obscenities and walked away. I removed some books from my locker and placed them in my backpack. Fooling with DJ had me running late. I wanted to be outside when Brenda pulled up because the sooner I got home, the sooner I could find out what was really going on with our parents.

Britney and Sierra waited for me near the exit doors. I told them about DJ. "You would have thought he had learned not to mess with us," Britney said.

Last semester, DJ tried to break up our friendship by making Sierra and I go up against one another. Thanks to Britney stepping in and showing DJ for the type of guy he was, our friendship survived. I was not trying to deal with his type of drama this semester. "Sierra, there's your mom," I said, pointing behind one of the school buses.

"Bye y'all. Call me tonight," she said.

Brenda yelled out my name. She sounded so country. Britney seemed to understand because when she looked at me, she said, "She's your sister."

"There's your driver," I said to Britney. The older man reminded me of the actor Morgan Freeman. He pulled up near Brenda's red Mustang. "What's up, ladies?" Brenda asked Britney.

"Nothing much," Britney responded. I ignored her.

"Tell your mom if she needs a babysitter for the twins, I'll be available."

"I'll let her know, but she'll probably hire a nanny," Britney responded.

I don't know why Brenda brought up the subject of the twins. After being a single child for fourteen years, Britney hadn't adjusted to the idea that her mom was pregnant. Britney was spoiled and used to getting all of the attention. After the twins were born, Brenda and Britney could compare notes. I'm sure Brenda's attitude toward me stemmed from the fact that I'm the baby of the family.

Britney left with her driver, Donovan, and Brenda and I headed home. I was not in the mood for a confrontation with Brenda, so I was relieved when she turned up the volume and we rode home listening to the loud music from her speakers.

"Mom, we're home," I yelled as soon as we entered the house.

"Act like you have some home training," Brenda said as she rushed past me up the stairs. I went to search for my mom. I ended up finding her in the living room staring at a blank television screen. Normally, she would have been dressed as if she was going to a video shoot, but she still had on her robe from earlier this morning and her normally styled hair was pulled up in a ponytail.

She patted the sofa for me to sit down. Her eyes were puffy and red. "Mom, are you okay?" I asked as I sat down by her.

She reached her hand out and covered mine. "I didn't want you to find out the way you did. I'll have to talk to Brenda about that later."

"Were you even going to tell me?" I asked, trying to control my voice level.

"Sweetheart, I was hoping that I wouldn't have to tell you anything."

"What happened? Why now? You've fought before." There were so many questions going on in my mind.

"Those are questions you need to ask your father."

"So you're telling me the divorce was not your idea but his?"

"Dear, what I'm saying is, some things you need to ask your father."

"But . . ." The realization of the situation hit me hard as tears flowed down my face. My mom wiped them away with her hands.

My mom sat straight up. "What happens between Dion and me is not a reflection of you, okay?"

"Mama, can you try to make it work?"

"Dear, it's not me. It's—"

Before she could finish her statement, my dad

burst into the room. "I can't believe you're trying to turn my own daughter against me," he yelled.

"Dion, it's not what you think." my mom yelled back.

"Jasmine, go upstairs because me and your mom need to talk."

"No. Stay where you're at," my mom said.

I didn't know what to do. I looked from one to the other. The tension in the room was at a volcanic level. The slightest shift in the wrong direction would have either one of them exploding. I remained seated and decided to defend my mom. "Dad, Mom was telling me I needed to talk to you about this divorce situation."

At six feet four and two hundred forty pounds, he could be intimidating, but I knew how to calm my dad down or so I thought. He sat on the other side of me. "I wished your mom would have waited to tell you, but since she didn't, yes, we're getting a divorce, but nothing is going to change."

"That's a lie." I could feel the insides of my stomach turning.

"Jasmine Charlotte, do not talk to your dad like that." Even now, my mom was taking up for him. Her actions were just a few of the reasons why I didn't think they should be calling it quits.

"You're still my favorite girl."

"Then why are y'all divorcing. See a marriage counselor. That's what Lala's parents are doing."

"It's hard to explain. When two people are going in two different directions like me and your mother, it's best to part ways."

"You told me not to be a quitter and here you are quitting at the first sign of trouble," I said.

"Life is complicated. It's not as simple as you might think." He looked at my mom to back up what he said, but she rolled her eyes and looked away.

I couldn't figure out why he insisted on leaving. "You have another family. Is that it? You've been cheating on Mom . . . on us."

"Kim, what other lies have you been filling her head with?"

"I haven't told her anything. Answer your daughter. Tell her the same lie you told me." If looks could kill, my dad would have been dead from the venom spurring from my mom's eyes.

He stood up. "I'm not going to deal with you like this. Not in front of Jasmine." He pulled me up off the couch. "Dear, I still love you. Don't let anybody—" he looked at my mom and continued—"tell you anything different."

I hugged him, not knowing if it would be the last time or not. I stood, watching him walk away. *If you love me, then why are you doing this? Why are you leaving me?* My mom sprang from the couch and looked out the window. I walked to the window and we both watched my dad get in his car and drive away.

We hugged each other. I found myself comforting my mom instead of the other way around.

3

I Need Love

I left my mom in the living room with her own thoughts. I didn't see a suitcase, so hopefully my dad left to cool off. I hoped whatever issues they were dealing with, they would resolve it and we could go back to being the happy family that I thought we were up until Brenda told me the real deal.

Brenda's door was cracked, so I walked in. "Didn't I tell you about knocking before entering," she snapped.

I was sick and tired of Brenda's attitude. It seemed the older we got, the more hell she tried to put me through. After Dad's dramatic exit, I was not in the mood. "I only came by to tell you that Dad walked out on us, but you're probably happy about that, aren't you?"

I didn't bother to wait on her response. I stormed out and went to my bedroom, locking the door because I needed to be by myself. I got Britney and Sierra on the phone and poured out my heart to them.

Britney, who seemed to be the most levelheaded out of the three of us, although I would never admit it to her, said, "If he didn't take any luggage, that means he'll be back. Give him some time to cool off. He'll be back."

"Y'all, what if this is really the end? Will we have to move? I don't want to have to choose who I want to live with."

Sierra responded, "Don't choose. Let them fight it out in court. By the time the courts figure it out, you'll be eighteen and then it won't matter."

"You got a point. Well, if they want to break up, I'm not going to make it easy for them."

"Y'all, I got to go. My mom is craving a roast beef sandwich and I'm the only one here," Britney said.

"Is she still on bed rest?" I asked.

"She'll be on it until she has the twins."

"Must be nice to have someone be at your every beck and call," Sierra commented.

"For some of us . . . but I'm on Mom duty, so it's rough on me," Britney responded. "Got to go, y'all, or else there'll be a mad mama on my hands."

We said our good-byes. "Sierra, you still there?" I asked after Britney hung up.

"I wish I knew how to help you," Sierra said.

"Well, I'm going to do like the pastor said last week and pray about it. There's nothing else I can do at this point," I responded.

Sierra cleared her throat. "Jas, I know we made up and things, but there's something I want to say about DJ."

"Nothing else needs to be said."

"I must or I'll never get it out."

"Whatever. Say what you got to say so we can move on."

"Jas, you win at everything, so when DJ showed me more attention than you or the other girls, I got the big head."

I agreed with her, but to keep the peace, I kept my comments to myself. "We're cool. DJ's a thing of the past, so drop it."

"I'll say this one thing and then I won't bring up his name again. I want you to know that I never stopped thinking of you as my sister. You and Bri are all I have. We'll always be friends so don't ever forget that."

Sierra caught me at a vulnerable moment. I refused to cry. I failed. "Sierra, I got to go. But we're cool. You'll always be one of my girls."

After the emotional day I had, I didn't feel like

doing any homework and I was too upset to go to sleep. I loved to shop when I was upset so I logged on to the Internet to order me some more lip gloss and a new outfit. It didn't take me long to do that so I decided to sign up to this chat room. After uploading a photo and signing up as DFWCutie, I logged on. It didn't take long before I started getting private messages.

MattBrn:	How old are you DFWCutie?
DFWCutie:	[I lied] 16.
TallandFly:	MattBrn, you're too old for her. She's more around my age.
MattBrn:	You're right. DFWCutie, be safe.
DFWCutie:	Bye MattBrn.
TallandFly:	DFWCutie I'm 16 too.
DFWCutie:	What school do you go to?
TallandFly:	Roosevelt High.
DFWCutie:	Cool. I go to Plano High.
TallandFly:	My cousin goes there.
DFWCutie:	What's his name?
TallandFly:	I would rather not say here.
DFWCutie:	Maybe you could tell me later.
TallandFly:	What's your e-mail so we can keep in contact?
DFWCutie:	Just click on my profile and leave me a message.

MattBrn:	You kids need to take that offline.
TallandFly:	We have every right to be on here.
ChatAdmin:	Sorry, but this chat is for 18 and over. DFWCutie and TallandFly, your profiles will be deleted.
TallandFly	send me your e-mail quick.
DFWCutie:	dfwcutie@dfwcutie.com

I was automatically booted out of the chat so I wasn't sure if TallandFly got my response. I surfed the Internet and came across casting calls for a reality television show. That's when the idea hit me. My dad practically admitted they didn't go to counseling. It didn't look like my mom really wanted the divorce. If I could get them help, maybe, just maybe, they would stay together.

I called Sierra back, but she didn't answer her phone. Britney answered on the fourth ring. I told her my idea. She responded, "I'm not sure your parents will be up for it. You better run it past them before submitting anything."

"You know if I ask, they are going to say no."

"But how are you going to submit their applications if they don't fill it out and sign it?"

"I'll fill it out for them and figure out a way to get them to sign it."

"I still think you should just drop it."

"One question: if it was your parents, wouldn't you do whatever you could to keep them together?"

Britney paused before responding. "Jas, you got a point. If you need my help, I'll help you."

I sighed. "That's exactly what I wanted to hear. I need you to ask Keith for access information to that background-check Web site."

"He's your cousin. Why don't you ask?"

"Because I don't want anyone to know what I'm up to."

"What's his number? You owe me one."

"I'll owe you more than one if all this works. Got a pen?"

I recited Keith's number to Britney. Soon afterward, we hung up. I was about to log off the computer when my e-mail alerted me of new mail from TallandFly. After a few e-mails, we logged on to instant messenger and we communicated that way until I got sleepy. TallandFly promised to send me pictures tomorrow and I couldn't wait. I needed a distraction from the drama going on in the McNeil household.

4

My Secret Friend

Usher was just about to kiss me on the cheek when Mrs. Johnson tapped on my desk. "Class is over, but you wouldn't know that since you slept through most of it."

I couldn't argue with her. I was a little sleepy from staying up on the computer the night before. "I had a hard night."

"Is there something you want to talk to me or one of the counselors about?" she asked.

"No. I think I'll be all right."

Surprisingly, she looked concerned. "If you ever need to talk, here's my number." Mrs. Johnson pulled out a business card and handed it to me.

I took the card and placed it in my backpack. Britney and Sierra were waiting for me outside the classroom door. "Girl, so how much detention did you get?" Britney asked.

"None," I responded nonchalantly and kept on walking.

They hurried up behind me. "See, told you she was the teacher's pet. If it would have been you or me, she would have given us some time," Sierra responded.

"Don't hate. Besides, I told her I was going through some things at home."

Britney and Sierra looked at me with a "yeah right" look on their face.

Before either could say anything, I said, "I'm not lying. I am going through some stuff."

"Try dealing with a pregnant mama," Britney said.

"Bri, it's not about you right now, okay."

Britney looked at Sierra and then back at me. She held up her hand. "Oh, no you didn't, Ms. Drama Queen."

The bell rang, indicating we were running late for our next class. Being tardy was one of the last things I needed. "Later," I said and rushed to my second class of the day.

I barely made it in time. "Jasmine, take one of those and have a seat," Ms. Lancelot, my algebra teacher, said.

My mouth dropped open when I realized it was a

pop quiz. I was definitely in trouble because I hadn't studied. Algebra was not one of my strongest subjects. The teacher had us grade one another's papers. Seeing the letter *F* at the top of my paper was not the best feeling in the world. I hated to admit defeat but I needed a tutor if I was going to pass the class by the end of the school year.

The rest of the morning went by in a blur as I fought to stay awake in each class. I couldn't wait for lunch just so I could take a nap. "Hey pretty lady, what's up?" some nerdy-looking guy asked as I headed to the lunchroom.

"Trying to get lunch," I responded and continued to the cafeteria. I was not interested in him because he was not my type.

Britney, Sierra, and I chatted over lunch. "This food is so bland," Sierra said as she took a bite.

"Maybe it'll make you lose weight," I said. Britney looked at me with her accusing eyes. "What? I'm just saying. Sierra says she wants to lose weight so what better way than to eat bland cafeteria food." I pretended that the vegetables on my plate had my full attention. I wasn't trying to hurt Sierra's feelings, but over the school year she had put on twenty-five pounds.

Sierra got up to get her some water. As soon as she was out of hearing distance, Britney said, "You can be such a jerk."

"I'm just telling the truth. You want me to lie to her?"

"Nobody said anything about lying. What you can do is be a little more sensitive and stop throwing up her weight every chance you get."

I put on some lip gloss and smacked my lips. "Believe me, I have other issues to deal with. Sierra and her weight are the least of them." Britney was not going to make me feel guilty about trying to look out for Sierra's health.

Sierra sat back at the table but didn't say much. My phone beeped. I saw that I had an e-mail. "Guess what, y'all? I met this guy." I couldn't wait to tell them about TallandFly after I saw his picture. It never dawned on me why he was e-mailing me in the middle of the day.

I passed my BlackBerry around so they could get a good view. "Isn't he adorable?" I asked, although I already knew the answer. He was tall and cute just like I like them. I guess I'm attracted to taller guys because my dad's tall.

"Where did you meet him?" Sierra asked.

"We met on this chat site," I responded as I typed a response, while we talked about him.

"My mom says chatting on the Internet is dangerous," Britney said.

"Well, it's not like he's a grown man or anything. He's seventeen."

Sierra gasped. "Seventeen is practically grown as far as our parents are concerned."

"Well, my parents don't care. They only care about themselves."

Britney threw her hands up in the air. "Here we go again."

"Well, he does sort of think I'm sixteen."

"Sixteen," Britney and Sierra blurted out at the same time.

"You didn't think I would give my real age, did you? I do look sixteen in my pictures."

"Girl, I can't believe you're talking to a dude that's seventeen." Sierra looked shocked.

"Sierra, I know we're not supposed to bring up his name, but DJ was sixteen and you didn't have a problem with his age."

"But that was different."

"Well, for me it doesn't matter. He's in high school. I'm in high school."

"What school does he go to?" Britney asked.

"Roosevelt High."

"Isn't that in South Dallas?" Sierra asked with her nose scrunched up.

"I don't know where it is. I know my mom went there when she was in school so it can't be all bad." I scrolled through my BlackBerry and deleted some of the e-mails from my new Internet buddy.

"Has your mom ever taken you back to her old high school?" Sierra asked.

"No. Why should she?" I leaned back in my chair and gave Sierra my full attention.

"Then something must be wrong with it because you know how your mama likes to brag," Sierra commented as she stuffed her face with more food.

I rolled my eyes. "I know you didn't say that about my mama, heifer."

Britney, forever the mediator, jumped in and said, "Sierra, chill out. Jas, she has a point."

My phone indicated I had another message. I checked it while I took a few deep breaths because I hated to go upside my best friend's head in public. I responded to TallandFly: My friends are getting on my nerves. I signed it *CWYL*—chat with you later.

"So when are we going to meet him?" Sierra asked.

I placed my BlackBerry on the table. "Try *n-e-ver.*"

"Hi, y'all. Bri, can I talk to you for a minute?" Marcus Johnson, DJ's cousin and Bri's ex-boyfriend, asked.

Britney looked at us and then back at Marcus. "We were in the middle of a conversation."

Not wanting to hear Britney lecture me, since I got enough of that from my parents and teachers, it was the perfect opportunity to push her off on someone else. "I got to go take care of something before the next class, so you two go right ahead and talk." I got up and looked back at Sierra. "Are you coming?" I asked her.

Picking up on the hint, Sierra got up. Marcus couldn't see Britney when she mouthed the words, *I'm going to get you.*

Sierra and I left the cafeteria. As Sierra and I parted ways, she said, "Be careful with that Talland-Fly guy."

After the fiasco with DJ, Sierra was the last person I would take boy advice from, but since I was working on being more sensitive to her feelings, I responded, "Don't worry. I know what I'm doing."

5

Baby Girl

After school, Britney's driver Donovan dropped me off at home to an empty house. I felt relieved that my mom wasn't lounging around having a pity party for herself; however, it didn't stop me from wondering where my parents were. Brenda, now, she could have moved to the other side of the world and I wouldn't have cared. Well, maybe just a little bit. Although we argued almost 24-7, I did love my sister. She gave good advice sometimes. Okay, most of the time, if I cared to listen to her.

My dad had my mom lay off some of the staff at the later part of last year due to the economy. My mom made it known she wasn't too happy about her now having to take on household duties that were normally done by other people. As long as I could still shop, I didn't have a problem with the staff being let go. I hadn't told my friends yet because I didn't want to be the only one of the three of us without a maid.

A brown envelope caught my attention as I walked by the living room. I looked around to double-check no one was around just in case they had come in while I was in another room. Some of the contents were spilling over to the outside of it, so it wasn't like I was about to look at something that wasn't opened. I glanced at the papers. They were legal separation papers but they were not signed, which meant I still had time to get them into counseling.

I rushed upstairs and called Britney. "Did my cousin give you the Web site information?"

"Let me check." Less than a minute later, she recited a Web site address and log-on information.

"Girl, got to go. I have to get this application filled out tonight so I can get it in the mail ASAP."

I hung up with Britney and logged on to the database and pulled up my parents' driver's license information. I wrote down all the pertinent information on the form. As I filled it out, I made it seem that they both were willing to work on the marriage, although I knew it was a lie. I couldn't see them turning down the application because I made sure I mentioned the fact that my dad was the former Super Bowl champion. An hour later, I was through filling out the questionnaires, responding to the questions the way I thought each one of my parents would. The only thing left for me to do was get their signature, giving the producers of the reality show authorization to move forward.

Since I was still home alone, I put the application to the side and tried to concentrate working on my homework. I logged on to our school's Web site to see who I could sign up with for tutoring. Soon after signing up for the tutoring information, I got a response giving me the details of the next tutoring session. My first session would be the next day so I placed the printed paper into my algebra book so I wouldn't lose it.

"Dinner's here," my mom shouted from down the hall.

My stomach felt relieved. I hid the papers under my books until I could think of how to get them to sign it and headed downstairs. Surprisingly, my dad was sitting at the table. I gave him a peck on the cheek. My mom entered the room carrying bags. "Someone could help me," she said, and I went to help her; but my dad remained seated. Brenda, frowning, waltzed in and sat down in her usual spot. My mom handed us each a black plastic container. She had gone to a local Italian restaurant and brought each one of us our favorites. My dad grunted when she handed him his container.

Tired of the silence, I said, "Dad, I'm glad you're here."

"Baby girl, like I told you yesterday, this is between me and your mother and doesn't have anything to do with you."

"Dad, you don't have to explain anything to her," Brenda said.

I rolled my eyes at her. "Anyway, I'm glad to see both of my parents here tonight."

"Can we eat in silence, please? I have a headache," my mom said as she sat down on the opposite end of the table from my father.

"You're always getting headaches, so that's nothing new," my dad responded.

Brenda looked at me as if she dared me to say something. We all rushed our food down. If anyone were to walk in the room, all they would hear was silverware tapping and folks chewing. After I finished eating my vegetable lasagna, I got up to leave.

"Jasmine, wait. We—" My dad looked at my mom and continued—"have something we need to talk to you girls about."

I slid back in my chair. My mom wouldn't look up from her half-eaten plate. "Dion, this can wait," she said.

"No, it can't." He paused. "You girls are old enough to know that sometimes things between parents don't work out."

"I refuse to do this." My mom threw her napkin on the table and rushed out the room.

Brenda followed her. I remained behind to see if my dad was going to say anything. His eyes that were filled with anger earlier now softened. "Looks like it's just you and me, baby girl."

I got up and sat next to him. "Are you leaving? Can you at least stay in the house?"

"Your mom and I can't keep fighting like this. It's not healthy. I don't want you to think this is how relationships are supposed to be."

"I thought you had a good relationship. I mean, all my friends' parents argue, so what's the big deal?"

"I know it might be hard to understand, but when two people fight as much as we do, the best thing to do is to separate."

"Okay . . . separate. Don't divorce. Maybe you two just need a cooling-off period."

For the first time in days my dad laughed. "Your mom wouldn't know the meaning of cooling off."

I looked my dad directly in the eyes. "Tell me the truth. Is it another woman?"

He moved his hand over mine. "Don't believe everything you read on the Internet."

I hadn't read anything on my favorite celebrity gossip Web site—the Young, Black, and Fabulous—about him. Up until his admission, I didn't realize he was being talked about on the gossip blogs. I made a mental note to Google him as soon as I got back to my room. "Then why, Dad? Why are you trying to leave us?"

"It's your mother I'm leaving, not you."

"But—but," I stammered.

"Look. I'll stay here until your mom and I can settle on a few things. But Jasmine, it's going to happen so you might as well get used to it."

"I can't believe you're doing this to us," I said over and over.

My dad got up and pulled me into his arms. He tried to assure me that nothing changed between the two of us. He repeated how much he loved me. Since he was feeling guilty, now was the time for me to make my move. I went upstairs and got the papers I needed him to sign. "What is this?" he asked.

"Something for school," I lied. I handed him a pen and showed him where to sign.

He didn't bother to read it and signed his name and handed the paper and pen back to me.

"Thanks, Dad," I said.

I found my mom in their bedroom. She was flipping television stations. Fortunately for me, Brenda was not around. "Are you okay?" I asked.

"I'm fine. What's that in your hands?"

"Just some papers I got from school. Dad's already signed," I said.

"I'm your parent too so why should he be the only one signing. Give it to me and show me where I need to sign," she snapped.

This was working out better than I planned. *Cool.* "Sure." My mom didn't see the smile forming on my face as she signed her name right next to my dad's. Operation Keep my Parents Together was in full effect.

6

The Fundamentals

I convinced Brenda to take me to the post office before dropping me off at school the next morning. I sent the documents priority mail so the show's producers would get them in two days. Our family needed this show so I hoped to hear from them soon. I put my cell number as a point of contact so I could intercept the phone calls. DJ and his friends were standing in their normal spot outside of the school. I ignored them as I made my way to where Britney and Sierra were standing.

Sierra tried to avoid looking in DJ's direction, but she failed to do so. Sierra, barely above a whisper, asked me, "Did you hear from your online man last night?"

"Girl, I didn't even check my e-mail. I had to deal with Dion and Lil' Kim."

Britney asked, "So did you fill the papers out?"

"Had them signed and put them in the mail before Brenda dropped me off."

"How did you get them to agree to the show?" Sierra asked.

"Well, I have my ways."

"You didn't tell them." Britney sounded shocked.

"What had happened was—" I stammered. Britney always had a way of making me feel guilty when I did something wrong. Not to say she was perfect, because she wasn't, but she did try to keep me on the straight and narrow.

"You better hope this doesn't come back to bite you," Britney said as she went on a mini-lecture.

I held my hand up. "Enough already. I'm just doing what I have to do to keep them together."

"But if they don't want to be together, they don't—"

I didn't let Sierra finish her statement. "Your parents are not talking about divorce so until they do, keep your comments to yourself."

Britney and Sierra made me so upset that I walked away. I didn't acknowledge them when they entered homeroom. I pretended to be reading my notes.

After homeroom, I rushed past them to my next

class. I was not in the mood to deal with them. Dealing with crazy parents was all I could take in one day. My BlackBerry vibrated in my pocket. I snuck and read an e-mail from TallandFly. I turned my Black-Berry off because I didn't want to get it confiscated. I wondered how he could text message me throughout the day. I'm sure Roosevelt High had the same rules we had. We could have cell phones but we weren't to use them during class. It was at the teacher's discretion on what to do if they caught us using them in class.

During my normal study hall period, I went to my first tutoring session. The nerdy guy I met on the hallway outside of the cafeteria the other day was the tutor. He smiled. I didn't. Maybe this was a bad idea.

"I'm Cecil." He extended his hand out for me to shake it.

"Jasmine," I responded. I barely touched his hand and he got excited.

"Maybe we can get to know each other better now that I'll be helping you with—" he looked down at the paper—"algebra."

I sat down at a table. "Look, Seal."

"It's Cecil," he responded.

"Cecil, whatever. I'm here to brush up on my math skills. Nothing more, understood?"

His eyes darted downward. "Yeah. I didn't mean to offend you."

"You didn't offend me. I just don't want there to be any misunderstandings."

For the rest of the study period, he went over the basics. We were scheduled to meet again tomorrow. "See, that wasn't bad, now was it?" he tried to joke, but I didn't find his joke funny.

I'm sure I would regret this later, but fifty minutes was not enough time for me to catch up on my math. I needed some more time. "Seal. I mean Cecil, what's your e-mail address and number just in case I have problems with my homework tonight."

He was more than excited to give it to me. In fact, he gave me several e-mail addresses. "If you can't reach me at that one, send an e-mail to this one."

"I don't need but one, but thanks." I took the sheet of paper and placed it in my backpack.

At lunchtime, Britney and Sierra were already seated at our normal table. I took a seat in my normal spot. "I guess the queen bee is talking to us again," Britney commented.

"You know your day would be incomplete without me in it," I responded.

"Incomplete of drama," Sierra jokingly said.

"Ladies, do you mind if I sit?" Cecil asked.

Britney and Sierra looked at me. I said, "In fact, yes, we do mind."

"Hey, I was just asking."

"Can't you see we're talking? So why are you interrupting?"

"Okay. I'm moving along." He looked like a sad little puppy dog as he hung his head and slowly walked away to a nearby table.

Sierra said, "You didn't have to be so rude to him."

"Nobody told him to come invite himself over either. He's tutoring me. I don't need to be socializing with him too."

"He's sort of cute," Britney commented.

Sierra asked, "Did you say *tutor*? When did this happen?"

"If you must know, I'm not doing so well in algebra. I hate to see my first semester grades tomorrow."

"You could have asked me. I'm good at math," Britney said.

"I know, but I needed someone who could be objective."

Sierra mimicked me. "Look at you, sounding all grown up."

"Whatever. I shouldn't have told y'all."

"I think that's a mature thing for you to do," Sierra

said. "You're taking action to make sure you do well in school. Your parents should be proud."

"They totally don't care about how I'm doing in school. Neither one has inquired about my report card yet."

"Well, we don't get them until tomorrow anyway."

"Still. They are so busy trying to get a divorce, they haven't bothered to ask me how I'm doing." I wouldn't admit it to my friends, but my parents' actions made me feel neglected.

"Don't worry about them. Things will work out," Britney said. She was always the optimist, but this time I think she was wrong.

Changing the subject, I said, "Guess what, that dude sent me another e-mail. He seems nice. I'm thinking about meeting him."

"Does he have any brothers or sisters?" Sierra asked.

"I don't know," I responded.

Britney asked, "Are his parents still together?"

"I'm not sure." I can't believe I didn't bother to ask him.

Sierra asked, "Does he have his own car?"

"I think so."

"Does he work part-time or is he just going to school?"

"We haven't gotten that far." By now, I was frustrated because they kept asking me questions I had no answers to. They acted like him and I had been knowing each other for a long time. I just met the dude so they needed to chill.

Britney said, "Then I think you should try to find out more stuff about him before you meet up with him."

Sierra asked, "Was it your idea or his idea to meet up?" I ignored her question.

"Promise me, you'll let one of us know when you do decide to meet up with him," Britney said, sounding more like a mother than my teenaged best friend.

"I want you both to be around when I meet him. I told you, I'm not stupid. He could look like a booger-wolf."

Sierra added, "Or worse; a mass murderer."

My skin crawled at the thought. I would definitely be asking him all the questions they asked me about him. I needed to learn as much as I could about my new Internet buddy.

7

Tall and Fly

The lunch conversation with my friends left me with a lot of unanswered questions. I didn't admit it to them, but I didn't even know TallandFly's real name. I only knew his screen name. I realized I had been hogging most of our chat conversations with things about me. Tonight when we chatted, I would be the one asking the questions.

Brenda was in her usual mood when she picked me up. "Mama thinks you'll go stay with dad if the divorce goes through," she commented on our ride home.

"Why would she think that?" I asked.

"You've always been a daddy's girl," she responded.

"That's not true. If anything, you're a daddy's girl. He always—and I mean *always*—gives you what you want."

"Yeah, after Mom lectures him."

"Oh, I get it. That's why you like to talk to me like you do. You're jealous. Jealous that when I came along I got the attention you used to get."

Brenda sped around our circular driveway and slammed on her brakes. My upper body jerked. Good thing I had on my seat belt or I would have flown out the window.

She turned around and started spouting out, "Look here, you little brat. I don't know what's going on in that little head of yours, but let's get something straight. You are nothing to be jealous of."

I didn't move because she surprised me with the anger she displayed. We argued plenty of times, but nothing like this. "Bren, calm down. I was just making an observation."

"What you need to be doing is figuring out who you will be living with, because, little girl, the divorce will be happening."

"It don't have to happen. I have a plan."

Brenda laughed at me. "Girl, the only plan you need to have is to figure out who you'll be staying with. As for me, I'm going with whoever pays my bills. I'm in college and I don't have time to be trying to find a job."

She left me in the car. I slowly gathered up my stuff and followed behind her. No one was at home but the two of us, and to avoid dealing with my feelings I decided to do homework. I called Cecil so he could help me with a few of my algebra problems. He was more than excited to walk me through. By the time we got off the phone and online chat, my algebra work was completed.

Before I could log off, a different chat-window session initiated by TallandFly popped open.

TallandFly: U Busy?
DFWCutie: Just finished some homework.
TallandFly: Perfect timing. Did U miss me?
DFWCutie: Of course [I flirted].
TallandFly: Good. Cause I missed U 2.
DFWCutie: But U don't know anything about me.
TallandFly: I know you're cute and sweet. Who wouldn't want to be with U?

[*True.* I could understand him falling for me already.]

DFWCutie: Thanks. ☺ What's your real name?
TallandFly: I was wondering when U would ask.
DFWCutie: I'm waiting.

TallandFly:	William
DFWCutie	That explains why U have Will.i.am's music on your site.
TallandFly:	So what's your name?
DFWCutie:	Cutie ☺
TallandFly:	Oh U got jokes.
DFWCutie:	My friends call me Jas.
TallandFly:	I'll call U Jazzy J.
DFWCutie:	U never told me if U have any brothers or sisters.
TallandFly:	U never asked.
DFWCutie:	I'm asking now.
TallandFly:	I have 2 brothers in college.
DFWCutie:	What about parents? R they still together?
TallandFly:	What's with the 20 questions?

[I hope I didn't offend him. I guess I could chill out and ask some more stuff later.]

DFWCutie:	I thought U wanted 2 get 2 know me.
TallandFly:	I do. 2 answer your questions, my parents are divorced.
DFWCutie:	Really. Mine are talking about divorcing.
TallandFly:	Too bad. How does it make U feel?

I wasn't sure if I should be telling this guy about my family problems. On second thought, Britney and Sierra didn't understand because both of their parents were together. He could probably relate more since his parents were divorced.

DFWCutie:	I feel like they don't care about me.
TallandFly:	I felt the same way.
DFWCutie:	Did your parents fight?
TallandFly:	Yes.
DFWCutie:	Lately, mine argue all the time.
TallandFly:	Maybe it's for the best.
DFWCutie:	I thought U was supposed to be on my side.
TallandFly:	LOL. Just trying 2 get U 2 see both sides Cutie.
DFWCutie:	I think they should try to work it out.
TallandFly:	If you think so, so do I.
DFWCutie:	You should see them. They are so cute together. They used to laugh all of the time.

I couldn't remember the last time they actually laughed together. Maybe on Sundays, but even then, I could tell it wasn't the same. If the reality show doesn't work out, then maybe I could get my pastor to talk to them.

TallandFly:	Cutie U still there?
DFWCutie:	Yes. I was just thinking.
TallandFly:	About me I hope.
DFWCutie:	I'm trying to figure out how to keep my folks 2gether.
TallandFly:	It'll work out.
DFWCutie:	How did you deal with your parents getting a divorce?
TallandFly:	I had two brothers helping me.
DFWCutie:	My sister Brenda's no help.
TallandFly:	I had friends too.
DFWCutie:	None of my friends understand what I'm going through.
TallandFly:	I'm your friend and I understand.
DFWCutie:	But, I'm talking about real friends.
TallandFly:	I can be your real friend if U let me.
DFWCutie:	I have enough friends.
TallandFly:	Everybody could always use another friend.

He had a point. He and I did have at least one thing in common. I wouldn't count TallandFly out yet. I needed someone to vent to as I dealt with the divorce that seemed to be staring me in the face.

8

The Phone Call

Britney had called my cell several times so I knew it must be urgent. "What's up?" I asked.

"Girl, your mama just left from over here. She was talking about your dad."

I swung the chair around with my back to the computer. Britney needed all of my attention. "What did she say?"

"Supposedly. Now don't get mad at what I'm about to say."

"Will you just spill it?"

"Well, your mom told my mama your dad is cheating. When she gave him an ultimatum—either the other woman or her—he chose the other woman."

Just what I suspected; it was probably one of those video-chicks-looking women that worked at his dealership. "Are you sure?" I asked, already knowing the answer.

"Yes. She didn't know who the other woman is but my mom said she'll help her find out. My dad walked in as they were discussing it and told her she was going to stay out of it. Your mom left because she didn't want to get my mom upset with her being on bed rest."

"Thanks, Bri, for letting me know." I hung up the phone with her. This was more serious than I thought. I shot TallandFly an e-mail. I was ready to talk to him off-line. I asked him for his phone number. He must have been sitting by the computer because he returned my e-mail quick with his number, 972-555-3424. I programmed his number into my BlackBerry, dialed star 67 and then dialed his number. I wasn't sure I was ready for him to have my number so I blocked it from showing.

"Hello," some guy said.

"Is this TallandFly? I mean, William."

"It's me, baby."

I loved the way he said the word *baby*. "This is Jas."

"Cutie?"

"Yep."

"I didn't expect you to call this quick."

"Well, I wouldn't have asked for your number if I wasn't going to call."

"Who are you on the phone with?" my dad asked, startling me.

"Got to go." I didn't wait for William to respond. I clicked the phone off.

"Somebody from school," I lied.

"How's school, by the way?" he asked as he sat on the corner of my bed.

"Okay, I guess."

"Make sure you keep your grades up. You might be able to get a scholarship."

"Did you lose another dealership?" He must have if he was concerned about me getting a scholarship.

"No, we're doing okay financially."

"It shouldn't matter how my grades are then, because you can afford to pay for it."

"Baby girl, some things will change and until the divorce is final, I'm not sure of what's what."

"So you're telling me when—I mean, if—y'all get a divorce you're not paying for me to go to college."

"Calm down. I'm still paying for your college, but with the economy, it might not be the college you want to go to."

"I'm supposed to go to Howard with Bri and Sierra. You promised me."

"Jas, settle down. That's three years away. I never said you weren't going. If you can get a scholarship at Howard, that would be great."

My dad was stressing me out. First him and my mama are getting a divorce and now he's talking like if I don't get a scholarship I won't be able to go to college. *Why is all of this happening to me?* I know what he's trying to do. He's trying to get my mind off the divorce, but that's not going to happen. If what Bri told me is true, then he had some explaining to do.

"Dad, I have a question and I want you to be honest with me."

"Have I ever lied to you?"

I looked at him with the *do you really want me to answer that* look on my face. "Did you cheat on Mom?"

The light in his eyes seemed to dim. His brown eyes darkened. "Guilty as charged, but it's not what you think."

Hearing him admit it knocked the wind out of me. I was expecting him to tell me it was one big misunderstanding. I never expected him to admit he had. It wasn't like he just cheated on Mom. I felt betrayed too. "How could you?" I asked, with tears flowing down my face.

He reached out to hug me, but I pulled away. "I didn't mean for it to happen. I love you girls. The pressure . . . your mom nagging. I just needed someone to talk to."

"You talk to Mom . . . not some skank," I yelled.

"Your mom and I have been having problems for years. It just escalated to this and that's why I know it's time for us to go our separate ways."

In between sniffles, I said, "Remember when I was a little girl, and how you would tell me that no matter what I could always depend on you. Well, you lied."

"I didn't lie to you. I'll always be there for you."

"You lied the moment you slept with another woman that wasn't your wife." I wiped off the remaining tears that were on my face and stormed out.

My dad rushed behind me. "Jas, don't walk away from me. We're not through talking."

"Go talk to your slut," I turned around and said.

He grabbed me by the shoulders. "Jasmine Charlotte McNeil, I am still your father and you will not talk to me like that."

Before I could react, my mother came up the stairway. "Get your hands off her now, you bastard."

She ran up to him and started hitting him on the arms.

"Mama, I'm all right," I said. "See. I'm all right."

"Dion, I can't believe you were going to hurt your own daughter. Isn't hurting me enough?"

My dad looked at my mom and then looked at me. "Kim, I wasn't going to—"

"I don't want to hear it. Dear, go to my room. I'll be there in a minute."

They argued in the hallway. The last thing I heard my dad saying was he was going to be sleeping in the bedroom downstairs. My mom cursed him out and then came to her room to make sure I was okay. "He didn't hit you, did he, because if he did, I need to take some pictures."

"No, Mama. He just grabbed me."

"I can't believe him. He knows how my daddy did me and I swore none of my kids would get beaten."

My mom didn't whoop us, but she sure didn't hold off on saying some words to you. After listening to her, sometimes you wished she would have whooped you so you could get the punishment over with.

"I'm really okay," I tried to assure her. My dad had pissed me off too. He had the nerve to grab me, when he was the cause of all of my problems. I guess both my mom and I were seeing a side of him we didn't want to see.

"I don't know why I still love that man. The way he's treated me and now his own flesh and blood."

I hoped the producers of that reality show didn't

take long to make their decision. The way things were going, I didn't have much time. Regardless of how mad I was at my dad, if my mom still wanted him, then it was up to me to do whatever I could to make it happen.

9

We are Family

"Jas, what are you doing here?" Brenda asked when she flipped the light on in her room. I sat up on her bed.

"We need to talk. I found out from Dad that he did cheat on Mom."

"What? Are you sure?" Brenda threw her purse on the table and plopped down on her bed.

"It came out of his mouth." I repeated to her what Britney had told me and also what our dad had confirmed. I also told her about him grabbing me.

"I can't believe he grabbed you," she said, sounding truly shocked.

"Neither can I." I rubbed one of my wrists. It still stung from earlier, but I didn't dare tell her or my mom.

"If I was Mom, I would kick his butt out."

"She still loves him, though, so why shouldn't they work things out?" I asked.

"Because once a man cheats on you, he'll do it again and again if you let him. I bet you it's not the first time."

"Why do you say that?"

"I remember." Brenda got up and shut her door. "You were only a few years old then. I think they separated then because he was caught cheating. Mama would never say, but I suspect that's what happened."

"Why didn't you ever say anything to me about it?"

"Duh. You were a little kid. You wouldn't have understood. Shoot. I didn't even understand it myself."

"He should have left us long ago then if we weren't enough for him."

"Silly girl, this isn't about you. It's about them. Him and Mom."

"I thought when you got married and had a family, you were supposed to take care of your family. Make sacrifices if you had to."

"Maybe he got tired of sacrificing."

"Mama still wants him, so I'm going to do whatever I can to help her."

"You go right ahead. He's my dad and all but he's still a man. If a man cheats on me, he is h-i-s-t-o-r-y—*history*."

"But—"

"No exceptions, as far as I'm concerned. Mama is the one who taught me that so I'm surprised she still wants him here."

"Maybe she forgives him."

"But you told me what Bri said. According to her, he chose the other woman. Mama needs to let the other woman have him and take Dad to the bank. In fact, I think I'll help her find a good divorce lawyer so she won't get stuck with nothing. I'm sure he had her sign a prenup."

"Bren, maybe if they got some counseling, their marriage could still be saved."

"Maybe, but don't count on it."

I left Brenda in her room surfing the yellow pages for divorce attorneys. Brenda was giving up on our parents but I refused to. No, what my dad did wasn't right, but if my mama was willing to forgive him, I would have to try to forgive him too.

I studied a little before logging on to the Internet. TallandFly sent me an instant message as soon as I logged on. I ignored him while I sent Cecil a question about my math homework. Cecil didn't take long to respond and confirmed I got a correct answer. William sent me another instant message. His impatience was the only thing I didn't like about him.

TallandFly:	U don't want 2 B my friend anymore?
DFWCutie:	Was busy.
TallandFly:	Can U Talk Now.
DFWCutie:	Why Do U Like Me?
TallandFly:	U are smart & pretty.
DFWCutie:	I am that.
TallandFly:	You're modest 2 I see. ☺
DFWCutie:	LOL
TallandFly:	So when can I meet u?
DFWCutie:	Soon.
TallandFly:	I can't wait.

We flirted back and forth. Sierra called me while I was online. "Girl, guess what DJ is up to now?"

I forgot all about William and gave her my full attention. "I thought DJ was an off-limit conversation between the two of us."

"I wouldn't be bringing it up if it wasn't important."

"Fine. What is the jerk up to now?"

Sierra blurted out, "He's saying you and him had sex and he has a recording to prove it."

This was the last thing I needed. I was already dealing with enough drama and now this.

"DJ better keep my name out of his mouth. In fact, let me call you back."

I blocked my number before calling DJ, but he didn't answer. I called Sierra back. "I need a favor. Call DJ on the three-way for me."

"But—" Sierra stammered.

"Please. He won't answer the phone and I know he'll answer if he thinks it's you."

Sierra paused, but did what I requested. DJ picked up after the third ring. "Yo, what's up? Sierra, I knew you would miss me."

"Trick, this is Jas. I heard that little rumor and if you know like I know you'll keep my name out of your mouth."

He laughed an evil laugh. "Jas, baby. You know you want me. I'm doing you a favor. Your stock has just gone up with the fellows."

"Screw you."

"According to me, you already did," he said while laughing.

I was beet-red. I clicked the phone off and threw it on the other side of the bed. A few seconds later, Sierra was calling me back. "What are you going to do?" she asked.

"I don't know, but you best believe DJ hasn't heard the last from me. He should have learned last semester that he can't mess with us and get away with it."

Brenda burst into my room without knocking.

"Girl, what's going on in here? I could hear you all the way on the other end of the hall."

"Sierra, let me call you back." I faced Brenda. "Remember that jerk DJ?"

"Yes, the one you almost let split up your friendship."

"He's at it again. This time, his target is me." I explained to her what Sierra had told me.

Brenda sat on the edge of my bed. Although we argued a lot, she was still my older sister and she was smart, especially when it came to guys. "Jas, from where I'm standing, this DJ guy has no credibility."

"What do you mean?"

"You all exposed him last semester for lying about things, so just because he's going around telling folks that you slept with him, it does not mean people will believe him."

"I know, but he's messing with my reputation."

"You know the truth so that's all that matters."

"What if I meet a guy who I really like and he believes the stuff DJ is going around saying. I don't want to be known as the school slut."

"As long as you carry yourself with dignity and not actually become the school slut, I don't think you'll have anything to worry about," Brenda assured me.

Brenda was right, but DJ was not going to get

away with trying to ruin my reputation. If it took me the rest of the semester to do so, DJ would not get away with it. I called Britney and Sierra to brainstorm. Operation Teach DJ a Lesson was now part of my agenda.

10

Parental Guidance

I strolled into class Thursday morning wearing shades, hoping Mrs. Johnson wouldn't make me take them off. My eyes were puffy from the lack of sleep. Between brainstorming with what we call "the lip gloss clique" and chatting with William online, I was tired. My mom's door was locked so I couldn't sneak some of her eye-repair makeup.

"Ms. McNeil, this isn't an awards show. Unless those shades are prescribed, they have to go."

"Yes, ma'am," I said, reluctantly.

The girl sitting next to me's expression said it all. I knew I looked a hot mess. The guy on the other side of me said, "Can she put them back on?"

Mrs. Johnson replied, "Thomas, I suggest you mind your own business and let me worry about the class."

A few snickers were heard around the room. I rolled my eyes at him and tried to pay attention to Mrs. Johnson as she went over the day's lecture. Before the class ended, she passed out our report cards. My heart raced as I tore open the envelope. I heard a few kids sigh in relief and a few sounded disappointed. I was scared to look at mine.

Mrs. Johnson said, "Make sure you return the signed copy of your report cards back to me on Monday."

I looked back at Britney. She was smiling so I assumed her grades were good. Sierra's smile was so wide, you could put an eighteen-wheeler in her mouth. I turned back around in my seat and slipped the paper out of the envelope. A, A, B, C, B, C and what I dreaded—a D in algebra.

I put my report card in my backpack. I had to pull my algebra grades up. I wanted to have at least a B average and at this rate, I had a long rode ahead of me. We shared our grades with one another after class was dismissed.

Britney teased, "I knew you were going to get an A in Mrs. Johnson's class."

"Me too," Sierra said.

"The D is what I'm worried about. It's messing up my GPA."

"Hey ladies," Marcus said as he walked up and stood by Britney.

We all acknowledged him. "I'll see y'all later," Britney said as she left to talk to Marcus.

Sierra said, "Girl, seriously, if you need some help in algebra, let me know."

"Cecil's a good tutor. He's actually better than my teacher."

By now, we were both standing at the door of my next class—algebra.

"Good luck," Sierra said, before walking to her next class. When it came to algebra, I needed all the luck I could get.

I walked in the room with my head hung low. I slipped into my chair in the back and waited for class to start. The teacher decided to talk about our grades. I wanted to hide under the desk.

"Some of you did exceptionally well. While some of you . . . let's just say, if you don't pull your grades up this semester, I'll be seeing you again next year."

A few grunts were heard throughout the room with some of them coming from me. Mrs. Evans handed out our new assignments. "This is due on Monday. If you need help, take advantage of the tutoring services that Plano High offers. See me after class if you have any questions."

I placed my paper in my notebook. I would be getting with Cecil later about my new assignment. The rest of my morning flew by. I accidentally bumped into Marcus on my way to lunch. "What's up with your cousin?" I asked.

Marcus threw up his hands. "I don't have anything to do with DJ so don't put me in his mess."

We walked toward the cafeteria together. I said, "Did you hear the latest rumor?"

Marcus didn't immediately respond. "I know it's not true."

"You know it and I know it, but some of these other people might not and that's what's pissed me off about the whole thing."

Marcus held the cafeteria door open. We got our food and walked past DJ and his friends' table. DJ shouted, "Man, why you walking with her. She's giving it up to you too?" Several of his friends laughed.

I stopped walking. Marcus said, "Don't let him get to you. Keep on walking."

I sighed and kept walking. I sat next to Sierra and Marcus sat next to Britney. I made a mental note to ask Britney about Marcus. He seemed to be hanging around her more than normal. They had broken up in the fall because of some misunderstandings caused by his cousin DJ, but maybe Britney was willing to forgive him. He was cool, but his stock went down just because he was related to the likes of Dylan Johnson.

I could barely eat my food as I watched DJ from the corner of my eye. Britney interrupted the evil thoughts going through my mind. "Are we still on for the weekend?"

"Of course." I didn't let Britney know that I had totally forgotten about our monthly sleepover. I'm too young to be stressed-out. At this rate, I'll have more gray hair than my grandmother. I pulled out my BlackBerry and sent my mom a quick text message. A few seconds later, she responded. She had forgotten too.

I typed, But Mom. It's our monthly and it's too late to cancel. Pleaseeee.

She responded, Okay, but you'll have to entertain yourselves. I don't feel like too much company right now.

I got her to say yes before she saw my report card. No matter what, I knew I would still be having the sleepover with Britney and Sierra. The rest of the day flew by. Leave it to Brenda to remember today was report card day.

"So how did you do?" she asked as soon as I jumped in the car after school.

"It was okay." She was not my parent so I didn't have to answer to her.

"I had straight As last semester so if you need some help with anything, your big sister . . . let's just say, I can help."

I buckled up my seat belt as she pulled away from the school's grounds. "I have a tutor for algebra already, so thanks but no thanks."

"Math is one of my strongest subjects."

"Everybody isn't like you, Bren."

"Hey, I'm just trying to be a good big sister."

I rolled my eyes as I pulled the sun visor down and put on some kiwi-melon lip gloss. "Have you seen Mom or Dad today?" I asked.

"Mom's not in the best of moods but Dad's walking around like he just won the lottery."

I put the sun visor back up. I was trying my best not to get depressed. Once we reached the house, I made a straight beeline to my parents' room. My mom unlocked the door. Her hair was all over her head. "Hey sweetie. How was school?"

"We got our grades today. I got a D in algebra," I blurted while I still had the nerve.

"That's good, dear. We'll talk more later. Mama was busy doing something."

Rewind. Did she just say that was good? Why was

she trying to rush me out of the room? Before I could go any further, my dad walked out of their bathroom with nothing on but his robe. Apparently, they had an afternoon rendezvous. I didn't know if that was a good or bad thing.

11

Reunited

I was in shock to see my dad in the room. Under normal circumstances, it wouldn't have been a big deal, but now seeing them in this intimate setting had me wondering if maybe they had changed their mind about the divorce. I hoped so.

"Jas was sharing her grades with me," my mom said.

"So how did my baby girl do?"

I handed him my report card. He viewed it. "Um-hum. I see," were all I heard coming out of his mouth. He then looked directly at me. "You did okay but you need to pull up your algebra grade."

"I'm already on it. I have a tutor."

My mom said, "I didn't know you were paying for a tutor, Dion."

"Kim, I'm not."

They both looked at me. "He's a kid at my school. It's a service they offer at Plano High."

My dad said, "I guess there are benefits to going to a public school after all."

Oh no he didn't. My friends and I should still be upset at our parents for taking us out of our private school and putting us in public school. Fortunately, the transition wasn't as rough as I thought it would be.

He signed my report card and handed it back to me. I listened to him give me a lecture on how important it was to get a good education. He gave me a black history rundown on how many people died and fought for me and my friends to be able to have choices.

"King, Booker T. Washington, Garrett Morgan, all of them were great men."

"Who is Garrett Morgan?" I asked.

"Our traffic lights are based on Morgan's designs. See, in this country, you can be whatever you want to be. Don't ever let anyone tell you anything differently."

"With President Barack Obama being our first black president, the door of opportunity is wide open for you, dear," my mom added.

My dad went on to stress the fact that he had to get

a football scholarship to go to college, but I had other options. February was coming up so I made a mental note of some of the names he told me about. In school, we always had to write reports during Black History Month. A lot of my classmates would probably choose President Obama to write about so I knew unless my name got chosen first I would need another option. I would look into the Garrett Morgan guy my dad told me about.

My fear of my parents splitting up was temporarily put on the back burner. I actually felt like we had a chance on staying a family. I left them alone so they could do what parents do behind closed doors. Maybe, just maybe, that would be the glue to keep them together. Brenda was in my room on my computer.

I rushed in. "What are you doing?" I asked. I hoped she wasn't being nosy, looking through my e-mails.

"My computer's acting up so I needed to look up something. Who is TallandFly?" she asked. I moved her hand away and typed my sister was on the computer to William.

"He's just a guy I met online."

She moved me out of the way. Brenda frowned. "Jas, talking to strangers on the Internet is not safe."

"He's not a stranger," I responded. I plopped down

on my bed and took out my homework. I wasn't sure how this conversation was going to go.

"Does he go to your school?" Brenda asked. Surprisingly, she wasn't being her usually bossy self, but actually sounded concerned.

"No. He goes to Roosevelt." I was feeling like I was on trial as many questions as she asked.

"Is he that guy that sits in the back at church that's always flirting with you?" Brenda printed out some information from the Internet for her class as we talked.

"Nope. That's Jeremy. Jeremy's a jerk so you don't have to worry about him ever getting my number."

"Then how did you meet him?" Brenda had a serious look on her face.

"Through a friend," I lied.

"Well, take it from me. Boys you meet on the Internet aren't always who they say they are."

I threw my notebook to the side. "Have you met some guys off the Internet before?"

"Plenty. Only one percent are worth talking about."

"What happened?" Brenda had sparked my interest.

"Most don't look like they say they do. If they say they're built, they're fat. If they say they are tall, they're short. If their profile says single, they are probably married with kids and I could go and on."

"What if they say—" I interrupted my own question. I wasn't ready to let Brenda know the truth about TallandFly. She would only try to talk me out of talking to him and I wasn't ready to stop doing that.

"Go ahead. If they what?" Brenda asked.

"Nothing. I was just curious. Where do you meet these guys you meet online?"

"I don't meet all the guys I chat with online but if I do meet them, it's always in a public place and I always—and I mean *always*—tell a friend where I am.

"You sure have a lot of questions. I thought you said a friend introduced you and this TallandFly boy."

"They did. But sometimes when I'm online, I chat with other boys. I just want to make sure I know the proper way to go about meeting them off-line."

"Your best bet is to stick to the guys you meet at school or at church."

"But what if—"

"No buts. Trust me. You're not missing out on anything, so stick to what you know."

Brenda gathered up her printouts and left me with my thoughts. TallandFly was still showing active online. I decided to ignore him until I finished my home-work. I scanned my problems that I had gotten from my algebra teacher and sent them to Cecil. Cecil called me.

"Meet me during your study period tomorrow and I'll show you the steps," Cecil said from the other end of the phone.

"Tomorrow's Friday. I need a break."

"Your assignment is due Monday but if we work on it during study hall, I think you can knock it out and still have your weekend to do whatever you girls do."

"It's a date," I said. "Not a real date, but you know what I mean."

He got quiet. "Jasmine. Thank you."

"Thank me for what?" I asked.

"For letting me tutor you."

"You're doing me a favor, so think nothing of it."

I hung up with Cecil and called Britney. "Girl, I think my tutor has a crush on me."

"That could be a good thing."

"I guess. I just need to pass algebra. I'm not look-ing for a boyfriend."

"What about that dude from the Internet?"

"William? He's just someone I pass the time with but you never know. But I didn't call you about that. My parents have made up."

"Really? When did this happen?"

I told her about my earlier encounter with my parents. Britney asked, "So you weren't grounded for the D in algebra?"

"All is well in the McNeil household."

12

It's Friday

Friday morning, I handed in my signed report card to Mrs. Johnson. She looked at the signature a long time as if she didn't believe it was authentic. She said, "Your dad made a good impression at the Christmas luncheon."

"He's just my dad to me," I said as I slipped into my seat. I was surprised Mrs. Johnson was starstruck. She didn't seem the type. Maybe Britney and Sierra were right; maybe I was the teacher's pet. If so, I would use it to my advantage.

"Class, today we're having a pop quiz."

Moans were heard throughout the class. Fortunately for me, I had studied so I passed with flying colors. I added another 100 points to my grades. The rest of the day flew by. I met up with Britney and Sierra after school. We piled into Brenda's Mustang.

"Mom said you can order pizza tonight. Her and Dad have plans tonight," Brenda said as she drove us home.

"Does that mean they are staying together?" Sierra asked.

I turned around to look at her. I forgot I hadn't told her about yesterday's encounter. "Let's hope so," I added.

Brenda said, "I don't know what's going on with them two."

I said, "I'm just glad they are talking again."

"Me too," Brenda admitted.

Beyoncé's latest song came on the radio. "Turn that up. That's my song," I said. Not waiting for Brenda, I reached down and turned up the volume. We all sang along and were pulling up into our driveway by the time the song ended.

Brenda went one way and the rest of us headed straight to my room. Britney and Sierra had been over enough to know where things were. About an hour later, we were all downstairs seated around the table eating the pizza Brenda had ordered.

Britney asked, "I want some dessert. Did your cook leave anything in the refrigerator for us?"

The moment of reckoning had arrived. I hadn't

told them about the house staff being let go at the end of last year. "Well, my parents let our cook go."

Britney and Sierra looked at each other; neither one knew what to say. Sierra broke their silence first. "My mom cooks for us most of the time so it's no big deal not having a cook."

"It sure isn't, Jas. So why the long face?"

"I thought you would look at me differently if I told you."

"Girl, please. We're all blessed, whether we have a cook, a maid or not," Britney said.

I could always count on Britney to be the level-headed one. It seemed as if I was worried for nothing. Life was good. My parents were hanging out together and I was hanging out with my friends. No complaints here.

Sierra polished my nails and added a cubic zirconia, to the tips. I put my hand under the air dryer. Britney was going through the latest issue of Flo Anthony's magazine and reading out loud the latest gossip. Britney said, "Do you think Usher and Tameka are going to have another baby?"

Britney knew Usher was my fantasy man so I don't know why she was trying to make me upset. "He's only with her because I'm not old enough. As soon as I turn eighteen, she can move over, because Jasmine will be in the house."

I reached up to give Britney a high five, but was interrupted when Sierra stopped me. "Your nails are not dry," she said.

"Well anyway, I love me some Usher."

"We know," Sierra and Britney said in unison. They liked to tease me about my fascination with the R & B singer.

We spent the next hour gossiping about our favorite celebrities. Britney pulled up a gossip Web blog and when I saw my dad's arm around some skanky-looking woman, I had to grab my head. "No, he didn't."

"Calm down," Britney said.

Sierra said, "It might not be what you think."

I scrolled down the page and read what the blogger said. I couldn't believe this. According to the blogger, the photo was as recent as earlier this week. I hoped and prayed that my mother did not see this picture, because otherwise these last few days were for nothing. I typed up a long comment and was about to hit the post button when Britney reached and turned off my computer.

"What did you do that for? Now I have to type all of that over again," I shouted.

"Girl, are you crazy? You know you can't say all of that. Only thing that's going to do is get folks to talking more."

My head pounded more and more. "I can't let them get away with it. My mom is going to have a fit."

"Let it die down."

"It's not. You saw it. They are tying that photo in to the application I sent that reality show. The photo and the show are two different things. Someone is always trying to stir up mess."

Sierra said, "Well, it could be a good thing. You wanted your parents on the show. If it's getting folks to talk already, the producers will probably go with them."

"But whoever leaked the information to the press need to have their behinds kicked."

"I'm used to it. They are always trying to tie my dad with this singer or that singer, but my mom and I know the real deal," Britney said.

Britney spent the next twenty minutes trying to calm my nerves down. Once she felt comfortable that I wasn't going to send out an online blast about the article, she turned the computer back on. William had posted several instant messages before I could respond. Sierra asked, "Doesn't he see that you're busy?"

"I'll let him know this is girl time so I'll chat with him later."

Britney said, "Chat now. Let's see what he's talking about."

DFWCutie:	Hi Will.
TallandFly:	What's up Cutie?
DFWCutie:	Just hanging out with some friends.
TallandFly:	Miss me?
DFWCutie:	Of course.
TallandFly:	Let's meet.

"What do I say? I'm not sure if I want to meet him yet," I asked as I looked from Sierra to Britney.

"I don't know about this," Sierra said.

Britney said, "Maybe you should just keep it on-line."

Decisions. Decisions. I typed my response.

| DFWCutie: | How about tomorrow? |

"Are you sure?" Britney asked.

"Yes, and you two can go with me."

Sierra said, "That's a good idea. That way we can check him out too."

TallandFly:	I can come pick U up.
DFWCutie:	No. I'll meet U.
TallandFly:	My mom will be gone so I'll give U directions.

"No, meet him at the mall," Britney said.

DFWCutie: Let's meet at North Park Mall.

It took him a few minutes to respond. "Maybe he got scared," Sierra commented.

"Oh well. I guess he didn't want to meet me after all." I was about to close out our chat session when his name popped up again.

TallandFly:	Sorry about that. My mom wanted me 2 do something 4 her.
DFWCutie:	So r U meeting me at the mall 2morrow?
TallandFly:	Can U meet me around one?

"If we can't get Brenda to take us, we can catch a cab," I said out loud.

| DFWCutie: | Yes. |
| TallandFly: | What will you have on? |

I looked at Britney. "I don't know what I'll wear. What do I tell him?"

Sierra said, "Tell him you'll be wearing something purple or orange. You have plenty of that in your closet."

DFWCutie: I'll be the girl in the purple. You
             already have my pic, so I shouldn't
             be that hard to spot. We can meet
             in front of the Coach store.
TallandFly: I'll see you then.
DFWCutie: What will U B wearing?
TallandFly: Jeans and I'll wear a purple polo
             shirt.
DFWCutie: So you like purple too?
TallandFly: It's my favorite color.
DFWCutie: Cool. Mine too.
TallandFly: What's your number?

"Can y'all hurry it up? I want to watch some videos," Sierra said.

I gave William my number before signing off. I turned and looked at my friends. "Ladies, it looks like we're going on a date."

13

Purple is Fly

"Wouldn't it be something if William is the one?" I said. I don't normally fantasize about ordinary guys, but William kept running through my mind.

"Don't rush into anything. Remember our pact," Britney said.

"I have no plans on sleeping with him. I just want to have fun. We seem to have a lot in common."

"Besides his parents being divorced, what else do y'all have in common?" Sierra asked.

"His favorite color is purple."

"You sure he's not gay." Britney laughed.

"Even if his favorite color was pink, it doesn't make him gay," I said. I didn't like being part of the punch line of their joke.

"He goes to Roosevelt. He's seventeen. His parents are divorced. I think that's all I know," Sierra said.

"And if you ask me, that's more than enough info," I snapped.

"Ladies. No arguing tonight," Britney intervened.

Sierra said, "I'm just trying to make sure we have all the facts so if something happens. . . ."

I interrupted her. "Nothing is going to happen. Besides, my two best friends—and that includes you, Sierra." She rolled her eyes but couldn't stop smiling. I went on to say—"Will be there with me when I meet him.

"What signal will you give us, if he's a jerk?" Sierra asked.

"Don't worry. I'll give you some sort of signal if I need you to come. Shoot, if he's ugly, I might just scream."

"Let's see his pic again," Britney said.

I logged onto my e-mail and pulled up his picture.

"He looks good on the pic," she noted.

"To me too," Sierra said.

"Brenda said most guys online put up old pics, so I hope he still looks good."

"He's only seventeen. In fact, that picture makes

him look older so he must have just taken it," Britney stated.

"I don't know. He didn't say," I responded.

Brenda stopped by the room and interrupted our conversation. "Mom and Dad aren't back. I'm about to head out with some friends. Are y'all going to be okay here by yourselves?"

"I'm not a child," I responded.

"You sure don't act like it," she teased.

"Just turn the alarm code on when you leave. We're cool," I said.

"See y'all later."

Before she could turn to walk away, I asked, "Can you drop us off at the mall tomorrow?"

"I don't know. What's in it for me?" she asked.

"I promise to not bug you for a week," I responded.

"Sounds like a deal. What time?"

"Around noon."

"Y'all better be ready too. Don't have me waiting all day on y'all."

"We won't," I promised.

Brenda left the room. "That's settled. Now I need to figure out what I'm going to wear."

Britney and Sierra watched me as I tried on various outfits. After about an hour, I decided on a pair of purple denim jeans and a satin purple top. I had a pair of white tennis shoes trimmed in purple that I had never worn.

"Good thing you're short, or you would be looking like Barney with all that purple on," Sierra teased.

"You just mad because the color doesn't look good on you," I shot back.

"Whatever, Ms. Drama Queen. It's getting late and I don't know about you two, but I'm about to go to bed."

Sierra yawning caused me to yawn. We said our good-nights. After they left to go to the guest rooms to sleep, I stayed up, hoping to hear my parents come in. The next thing I realized, the sun was shining through my bedroom window. I woke up to the sounds of birds chirping.

I heard a light knock on the door. "Come in," I said, as I wiped the sleep from my eyes and sat up in the bed.

My mom, fully dressed in jeans and a shirt, walked in. "So how did it go last night?" she asked, sounding like she was in a good mood. She sat on the edge of my bed.

"We just hung out and do what we always do."

"Good. Well, your dad and I will be going to this benefit tonight so you can order dinner from wherever you want."

"Cool. I'll just charge it."

My mom sat on the edge of the bed and said, "Jas, your dad and I have been talking."

"You're remaining together," I said. I got out from under the covers and hugged her.

"Hold on. We're taking one day at a time."

"What about that other woman?" I asked.

My mom's eyes looked away. "Don't worry yourself about that. She's not an issue."

"But—" I said.

"No buts. I got it all under control."

To me, she didn't seem too confident, but hopefully she was. We chatted for a few more minutes and then I got up to bathe. She surprised me by cooking breakfast for us. My entire family, including my friends, sat around the table and talked like it was old times. My dad loved being the center of attention. I glanced at my mom to see how she was doing. She seemed to be doing okay, but something wasn't right. I could feel it in my guts.

By the time we cleaned up the kitchen, it was time for us to head to the mall. I called William before we left and he assured me he would meet me around one. "Let's go," I said as they waited for me at the bottom of the stairway.

For January, the weather was unusually warm, so Brenda wanted to let the top down. I couldn't let her know I was meeting a boy, so I coughed. "That might be too much air on me," I said.

"If you weren't feeling well, you should have stayed at home," she said.

"I'll be all right. If I get tired, I'll sit and wait on them two to finish their shopping."

Traffic on Central Expressway was the normal Saturday traffic. We listened to music all the way to the mall. She pulled up in front of the Dillard department store entranceway. "What time do y'all want me to pick you up?"

I chatted with Britney and Sierra to see what time. "You can pick us up at the bookstore across the street around six," I said.

"Don't have me waiting all day because I have a date tonight."

"So you're headed to the beauty shop now?"

She glanced in the mirror. "Why? Something wrong with my hair?" She ran her hands through her thick, curly hair.

"It looks good to me," Sierra said.

"Y'all sure? Because this guy is fine and I need to make sure I look good tonight."

I glanced at my watch. Time was of the essence. "Bren, you're blocking traffic. We'll see you at six," I said as I led Britney and Sierra away from the curb. "I thought she would never go," I said once we were out of earshot.

"Are you nervous?" Britney asked.

"Who, me? I'm purple fly, of course not," I lied.

I followed my friends into the mall's doors. It was time to meet TallandFly.

14

Disappearing Act

The Coach store was packed. I didn't need a new purse, but it was fun to look at the new collection. I didn't have much time to look because it was almost one o'clock. I vowed to stay within clear-eye view so if William was not the type of guy I wanted to hang with, they were to come to my rescue.

Britney said, "It's time."

"I know." I glanced in one of the mirrors on the wall in the store. "I hope he's cute."

"He will be," Sierra said.

I glanced around the mall in both directions when I walked out the store. I didn't see anyone who resembled William's picture. I took a seat on one of the benches at an angle, so I could view my surroundings. I looked in the direction of the store and Britney waved. I acknowledged that I saw her by moving my head up and down.

My cell phone rang. It was an unknown number but I answered anyway. "Jas, it's Will."

"Will, where are you?" I asked.

"I'm almost there. Where are you?" he asked.

"I'm waiting for you outside of the store like we planned."

"Are you wearing purple?"

"I told you I would have on purple," I responded.

"I'll be there in about twenty minutes. My bus was running late."

"Call me when you get here."

Frustrated and disappointed that I would have to wait, I went back to where Britney and Sierra were shopping. "He's late," I said, before either could ask me a question.

"Well, that just gives us time to go to the M•A•C store."

"You two go ahead. I'll wait around here. I don't want to miss him."

"We can wait with you," Sierra said.

"You know what. Who cares if he knows you guys are here. He should have been on time."

"He would have to meet us eventually anyway, so it might as well be now," Britney stated.

We sat and watched people as they walked by. We

joked and without me realizing it, over thirty minutes had passed by. There was still no sign of William. I checked my phone to make sure I had a reception. I checked my text mail and voice mail but there weren't any messages from William. I stood up and walked away from where my friends were sitting. I called William. He answered on the second ring. "Where are you?" I blurted.

"I didn't know you were bringing your friends," he responded.

"So you were here and didn't say anything," I shouted into the phone. I clenched my hands.

"I'm shy and I don't like to be around a lot of people."

"That's bull. You could have come up to say hi. My friends would have gone to do something else."

"Let's try to meet another time."

"No. It's either now or never," I responded.

"I'm already outside trying to catch the bus. In fact, the bus just pulled up."

"William, if you get on the bus, don't worry about trying to meet me again."

"Jas, I don't want to meet your friends right now. I'm trying to get to know you."

"My friends and I are a package deal."

"Okay, for you, I'll make the exception."

"What exit are you near and I'll meet you there?"

"I'm on the east side of the mall," he responded.

"Don't go anywhere. I'm headed that way now."

"By yourself?" he asked.

I didn't answer him and clicked my phone off. I walked up to Britney and Sierra. "Come on, he's on the east side of the mall. I need you to fall back behind me, though. He saw y'all with me and chickened out."

Britney said, "I don't like the sounds of that, Jas. Maybe we should just go to the bookstore. I can call my driver Donovan and you can call Brenda to let her know we don't need her to pick us up."

"I've come this far, so I might as well meet him."

By the time we got to the east side of the mall, I saw people getting on a bus. I looked around to see if I recognized any of the faces near the entryway. I walked outside of the mall and noticed someone waving at me from the tinted windows of the bus. At a glance, that had to be William. "Why did he leave when I told him I would meet him over here?" I asked out loud.

I dialed his number and he picked up. "Get off the bus."

"I can't. I don't have enough money and the driver is not going to give me a refund."

"Fine," I said as I clicked off my phone. I was mad because I felt like he stood me up in front of my friends. I went back inside by myself. "Remind me to never meet another boy off the Internet," I said and kept walking past Britney and Sierra.

They caught up with me. "What happened?" Sierra asked.

"He got on the bus. Some excuse about not being able to get a refund and he couldn't afford to get another ticket."

Britney said, "Well, Jas, everybody can't afford stuff like we can, so give the guy a break."

"If he wouldn't have been so shy, we could have met. He could have at least said hi face-to-face before leaving."

"Did you at least get a good look at him before he got on the bus?" Sierra asked.

"He was already on the bus. The windows were tinted, but it was him. He waved."

"Maybe, now wasn't the time. Calm down, there will be others," Sierra said.

"I don't know if I want it to be a next time. If he can't afford a bus ticket, he's not going to be able to afford me."

"Now that is so shallow," Britney said.

"You can't tell me that you would date a guy without money."

"Hello. I dated Marcus."

"Marcus doesn't count. His parents aren't rich, but they sure aren't poor either."

"Okay, Marcus wasn't a good example, but to me it doesn't matter."

"I'm not a gold digger, but if he can't at least have money to ride the bus, he and I might have a problem."

"I know that's right." Sierra said, giving me a high five.

"I don't know about y'all but I'm hungry." William had stressed me out. I had forgotten all about looking into being a vegetarian. I wanted some meat.

"Le Madeline's right around the corner," Britney said.

"I want a chicken sandwich with the works," I said.

Time passed by fast after we ate. After going from store to store in the mall for a few hours, we went to the bookstore across the street. We each bought a copy of the latest book in the *Denim Diaries* series. Britney would probably beat us both reading, but I was determined to read it as soon as possible because I didn't want her to tell me how the book ended.

Brenda was all too happy that she didn't have to wait for us when she pulled up. She rushed us home so she could get ready for her date. My parents had already left for their charity ball. I ordered food and had it delivered. It arrived shortly after Brenda left.

My phone beeped. It was William. "You can't keep avoiding him," Britney said.

"Watch me." I clicked the off button on my phone and threw it on the couch. I might talk to William later, but not tonight. He should have talked to me earlier when he had the chance. I'm taking a page out of Brenda's book—*next*.

15

Parents Behaving Badly

We ate in the den and sat on the long brown sectional. We spent the night watching some of our favorite movies and ended up falling asleep where we sat. Our naps were short-lived when we heard the sounds of my parents' voices down the hall. "Dion, how could you embarrass me like that?" I heard my mom say, as I heard a door on the first floor slam.

Sierra stretched and wiped her eyes. "That movie sure is loud."

"Shhh. That's my parents," I said, hoping they didn't hear us.

My dad knocked on a door hard. "Kim, open that door or I'll bust it in."

My hand flew to my mouth. Britney said, "Maybe we should go upstairs."

"I'm not going anywhere. I want to know what happens and if I go upstairs, I'll never know."

So we eavesdropped on their conversation. "You knew your other woman was going to be there and you had me looking stupid."

"For the umpteenth time, I had no idea she was going to be there. Do you really think I would have had you go with me if I knew that?"

"I don't know, Dion. Lately, you've been doing some strange stuff. I wouldn't put it past you."

"Look. Those girls are upstairs and if you don't stop this nonsense you're going to wake them. They don't need to be hearing all of this."

"I'm sure Jasmine has told them we were having problems," she yelled back from her end of the door.

"Still. Come on, Kimmy. I'm trying to work with you here. We were doing fine."

"Yes, until your skank showed up and ran in your face."

"I can't control that."

"Just like you couldn't control what's in your pants."

"I'll let you calm down. I'm going upstairs."

It sounded like someone was coming in the room where we were, so we rushed back to the sectional couch and pretended to be sleep. My mom said, "Girls, you can stop faking. I know you didn't sleep through all that."

My mom stood in a black knee-length evening dress. Her eyes were puffy from crying. "Mom, you all right?" I asked, as I got up to hug her.

"I'm fine. Your dad and I just had a little disagreement. All will be well tomorrow. Bri and Sierra, sorry you had to witness our little family drama."

Neither knew what to say, so they looked away. I was so embarrassed. Britney said, "We'll see y'all in the morning."

They left me alone with my mom. She tried to apologize to me for the mishap. "No need to apologize, Mom. I've seen their parents argue before." I had, but nothing like what they were doing.

It seemed the stairways had extra stairs. I was beat by the time I got to the top of the stairway. My weekend started off filled with promise, but now I felt things were crumbling. I tossed and turned throughout the night. Every time I fell asleep I had a nightmare about my dad taunting us with his other woman.

With the drama from the previous night, I was surprised to feel someone shaking my bed Sunday morning, saying, "Wake up, Jas." My mom stood over me dressed in her robe.

"What time is it?" I asked.

"It's nine o'clock. If you hurry up, we'll make it to the eleven o'clock service."

Barely awake, I responded, "We still going to church?"

She responded, "The Lord doesn't stop working because we have issues, dear."

"I know. But I haven't gotten all my sleep in." I fell back on the bed.

"Take a nap later. Your friends are already getting ready."

"Okay. I'm getting up," I said, sluggishly. Less than an hour later, Britney and Sierra were knocking at my door.

"That's a pretty dress," I said to Sierra.

"Thanks. I got it from Old Navy."

"Sorry y'all about last night," I said.

"Don't worry about it," Britney said.

Brenda yelled, "Mama said, hurry up."

"One of you can sit up front if you like," I said as we headed downstairs.

"It's your mom. You sit up front," Sierra said.

We were all in shock when we got outside and saw my dad behind the driver's seat of the SUV. My mom came rushing behind us. "Come on, ladies, we're already running late. We'll be sitting in the nosebleed section."

We sent each other text messages because other than the gospel music my dad blasted from his speakers, they weren't talking. The parking lot was full by the time we made it to Saint John Missionary Baptist Church. My father let us out. "You girls go ahead and find a seat. I'll wait for your dad."

"Mom, I thought—"

"Dear, now is not the time," she interrupted me before I could finish my statement.

Britney said, "There go my parents." We followed her to the middle of the church and greeted each other.

Mrs. Franklin looked like she was going to have her babies sooner than later. "You girls have been behaving yourself, haven't you?"

"Yes, ma'am," Sierra responded.

"Jasmine?"

"Yes, ma'am."

"How's your mom?"

"She's fine. They're around here somewhere."

"They?" she responded.

"Mom and Dad."

From the look on her face, Mrs. Franklin was shocked. An usher came along. "Girls, you need to go find your seat. Services will be starting in a minute."

Mrs. Franklin looked around. "You have my permission to sit in the balcony. I'll see you after service."

Britney said, as we were walking away, "Where else was I going to sit?"

"Bri, I can't believe you're mouthing back at your mom and in church."

"Well, I'm just saying and besides. I'm not being disobedient. I was just stating a fact."

We sat on the front row of the balcony and had a good view of the choir and pulpit. We stood as Pastor Hayes and the rest of the ministers entered the pulpit. The deacon said a long prayer and Sierra had to nudge me because I had dozed off. I hoped I wasn't drooling. I used a tissue to wipe my mouth just in case.

One thing about being in the balcony, our parents weren't around to tell us to stop talking or passing notes. We did that most of the service. Some of the other adults sitting nearby gave us funny looks. We would look at each other and temporarily stop but would start right back up. I just hoped none of the parents knew our parents.

Pastor Hayes preached about people faking and how the Lord didn't like hypocrites. I stopped passing notes so I could pay more attention. I thought about my parents' situation. They came to church as if all was well, but in reality, there was turmoil in our house. I felt like Pastor Hayes was talking about my parents. I knew they were faking because they could barely say two words to each other earlier. My dad needed to get it together. I was supposed to look up to him as a role model, not think of him as a hypocrite.

16

Rescue Mission

"I'm going down there," I said as the pastor asked people who needed prayer to come to the front.

"You want us to come with you?" Sierra asked.

"Nope. This is something I have to do for myself."

I left them upstairs and went down to altar call. There were several other people headed down the aisle, but I didn't care. I heard my mom call my name when I passed her pew, but I didn't turn around. I knew if I did, I probably would lose my nerve so I kept on walking. When I reached the end of the aisle, I stood and waited for the pastor to get to me.

Tears were flowing down my face by the time Pastor Hayes made it to me. "Young lady, tell everybody your name and why you're here."

"Pastor Hayes, my name is Jasmine and I'm here because I need some divine intervention."

I heard a few *praise Gods* coming from various areas of the church.

"Well, Jasmine, you came to the right place. Because the Lord I serve can handle any situation."

"Amen, Pastor," someone in the congregation said.

"Whatever your problem is, give it to God."

Before I knew it, I was crying more. "We're going to pray right now for this young sister. Lord, you know what Sister Jasmine is going through. You're a God who sits high but looks low. Our sister has stepped out on faith and has come to you asking you for help with her situation. Let her know that even if her prayer isn't answered in the way that she would like for it to be, that you will not abandon her in her time of need. That her coming to you in her time of need is an invitation for you to do miraculous things in her life."

The pastor hugged me and it felt like the load had been lifted from me. He said, "Sister Mae Pearl, come take this young lady and talk to her. If she needs more prayer, pray with her."

The deaconess came and wrapped her arm around me and led me out a side door into the hallway. She prayed for me and asked me if I needed to talk about anything. My mom rushed behind. "Jasmine, baby, you okay?

"Sister Mae Pearl, I appreciate you talking to my baby girl, but I got it from here."

The deaconess looked at me for reassurance. I nodded my head that I would be okay. My mom wrapped her arms around my shoulder and we walked toward the bathroom. "I didn't know this situation was getting to you like this."

"Mom, I love you and Dad. I don't want to choose who I want to stay with. I want us to remain a family."

"I'm trying. I'm trying my best, but I don't know how much more of your father I can take." She began rocking back and forth. I hugged her tight and I'm not sure how long we were in front of the bathroom hugging each other, but we didn't move until several people came into the hallway saying, "excuse me."

My mom reached in her purse and pulled out a few tissues. We wiped our faces. She ran her hand through my hair and patted me on the cheek. "Let's go find your father and friends and get out of here."

I followed her back into the main sanctuary. The pastor was still shaking hands. "You all right, sister?" he asked as my mom and I got near.

"Yes, Pastor. Thanks for praying for Jasmine."

"There's no problem too big for the Lord," he stated.

He gave us both a hug and we continued on to our destination. My dad, surrounded by a lot of men, was waiting for us outside. They were busy talking about the upcoming Super Bowl. I looked around to see if I could see Britney or Sierra because the adult's conversation wasn't of interest to me.

My cell phone vibrated. I checked it to see if it was one of them letting me know where they were. It was William. I deleted the message without looking at it. He could give it up. I was no longer interested in him.

"Girl, you okay?" Britney asked me.

"I'm fine. I just needed to get that off my chest."

Sierra said, "We're here for you if you need to talk."

"I know, but only God can help with this problem."

We chatted until my dad motioned for us to follow him to the car. With my heels on, it seemed as if he was parked two miles away. By the time we got to the car, all of us had our shoes in our hand.

"I don't know why y'all wear those high heels anyway. When I was growing up, girls your age wore cute little black patent leather shoes."

"Daddy, that is so old school."

"Old school? Did you hear that, Kim? We're old school now." He started laughing.

She responded, "They are talking about you. Because I always keep up with the latest fashion."

I rushed to change the subject. "That was a good sermon Pastor Hayes preached today, wasn't it, Daddy."

He looked over at my mom and then in his rearview mirror at me. "It sure was. You made me shed a few tears when I saw you walk down that aisle."

We talked about the sermon until we got to Pappadeaux, a local seafood restaurant. The normal Sunday crowd was there but we didn't have to wait like some people. It was a perk of being the daughter of a local hero. My dad signed a few autographs along the way.

"Come on, ladies. He'll be awhile," my mom said.

Sometimes it seemed as if my mom was jealous of the attention he got, but as long as they had been married, she should have been used to it. The waiter was bringing our appetizers by the time he made it to our table. "Sorry about that, ladies. Everybody wanted my opinion on who I think is going to win the Super Bowl. You know I have to go with my Cowboys. I'll be a Cowboy until the day I die."

My mom muttered, "Can we stop football talk for one day?"

"Yes, dear." With a surprising move, my dad got up and kissed my mom on the cheek.

We all pulled our menus up closer to our face as if

we didn't notice his gesture. Two waitresses rushed over to our table as soon as they realized Dion McNeil was at the table. "Is there anything we can get for you?" one of the young ones asked.

I said, "I would love a refill on my lemonade."

She ignored me. "Dion," my mom yelled.

"Yes, my daughter would like some more lemonade. In fact, could you bring more drinks for everybody?"

"Sure, Mr. McNeil."

It was hilarious watching them make a fool of themselves. My mom didn't find it too funny though. All eyes were on us as we ate dinner—nothing unusual for the McNeils.

After dinner my dad dropped Sierra and Britney off. He insisted on speaking with each of their fathers so between the time we left the restaurant and the time we dropped each one of them off, it took an hour. They had to wake me up so I could get out of the car once we made it home.

"I can't carry you like I used to. This old man's back would go out."

"I'm not that big," I said.

"No, half-pint. You're still cute as a button too."

My dad knew how to throw it on thick. He made it hard to stay mad at him. Feeling sluggish, I tried my best not to go to sleep because otherwise I would end up being up all night. I chilled in the living room and watched television.

Brenda plopped down on the sectional across from me. "I guess your little stunt at church worked. They are in their room doing grown-folks things."

"First of all, it wasn't a stunt and secondly, that's nasty."

"I had to come downstairs because they were keeping up too much noise."

I shook my head. "Gross." I smiled because it seemed Operation Save My Parents was working.

17

A Bug A Boo

Every time I got a text message from William, I thought about the song by Destiny's Child. He was surely becoming a bug a boo. It was after nine on Sunday night and he had sent me at least twenty text messages since this morning. I decided to call him and tell him one last time that I didn't want to speak with him anymore.

"William, I don't how many ways to say this, but dude, stop calling me."

"Jas, I told you I was sorry. I'm shy. Your friends scared me away. Give me one more chance. Please."

"No. Go find someone else to bug."

"But I love you."

"Love me. You don't know me to love me."

"I know all I need to know. When I saw you sitting there in that purple, I wanted to hug and kiss you."

"Dude, I'm glad you didn't because you would have gotten slapped."

"Can't you understand?"

"Look, William. We can still be friends. Every now and then, if you see me online, shoot me a message. But otherwise, you need to chill on the text messages."

"Jasmine, I love you."

"What?" He had to be kidding. He totally caught me off guard with his response.

"I want to see you again. This time I promise I won't run away," he groveled.

"William—if that's really your name—I am going to hang up this phone and we're going to pretend like this conversation never happened," I nervously responded.

I didn't wait for him to say good-bye. I hung up and called Britney and Sierra on the three-way. "This guy doesn't even know me and he's talking about love. I'm so glad that he got on that bus."

"According to you, you do have that effect on guys," Sierra teased.

"I wasn't serious. I mean, I know it's possible because I am me, but he only saw me one time and now he's talking about he loves me," I said.

"If he keeps texting you, just get your number changed," Britney suggested.

"I don't think so. You must have forgotten that when your dad had that album release party and I met Soulja Boy that this is the number I gave him."

Britney laughed. "Girl, if Soulja Boy hasn't called you by now, he's never going to call you and I mean *never*."

"You're just jealous because he danced with me and not you."

Sierra said, "He had no choice. You practically dragged him on the floor. He was trying not to embarrass you."

"So many haters on the phone. Y'all just haters," I said jokingly as we continued to reminisce about the party Britney's father got us invited to a year ago.

"Britney, you still on the phone?" I heard Mrs. Franklin say in the background.

Britney rushed us off the phone to see what her mom wanted. We said our good-byes and hung up. Sierra said, "I'll send you the instructions on how to block William from sending you messages online."

"Please do. I'm about to log on now and I really don't want to keep hitting cancel all night on his instant message requests."

Sierra walked me through setting up the block but not before William had sent me ten messages. I responded once asking him to get a life. "It's done. Thanks, girl."

I wasn't online long after Sierra and I got off the phone. It was kind of boring not having anyone to chat with. I guess I was having TallandFly withdrawals. I fell asleep at the computer.

"Do I need to confiscate your laptop, young lady?" my dad asked the next morning when he found the laptop on and lying next to me in the bed.

"No, Dad. I don't know what happened. One moment I was playing a game and now here you are."

"You're running late. Brenda had to leave because she has a test, so I'll be taking you to school this morning. Hurry up so we won't have to hear your mom's voice."

"Is she up?"

"Uh, no. She's still sleeping so that's why I need to get you up and out of here before she does wake up."

Less than an hour later, my dad was pulling up in front of a drive-through so I could get breakfast. I ate while we listened to *the Tom Joyner Morning Show*. Some of my friends thought the show was old school, but because of my parents I liked old school music and besides, his show has some of the best celebrity interviews.

"Brenda will pick you up like she normally does,"

my dad informed me as he dropped me off in front of the school.

I kissed him on the cheek and rushed to homeroom. I barely made it in time. I wrote a quick note to Sierra and Britney since Mrs. Johnson wasn't in class yet. A man walked in carrying a briefcase. There was something familiar about his eyes. "Hi, class. I'm Mr. White. Mrs. Johnson had an accident and couldn't be here today, so I'm your substitute teacher."

After class, Mr. White said, "Jasmine, do you mind staying afterward?"

"Sorry, Mr. White, I have to go to the bathroom and I can't be late for my next class." Mr. White's demeanor made me feel uncomfortable. I don't know if it was his wicked smile or the creepy way he looked at me.

I rushed out. Britney said, "I wonder why he wanted to see you."

"Me too," I said. I looked over my shoulder. For some reason I was expecting him to be in the doorway watching, but he wasn't. It must be my lack of sleep getting to me.

18

The Formula

"Cecil, you're the greatest," I said as I walked into the study hall waving my A paper from the pop quiz we just took in algebra.

"I'm glad I could help." He took it from me and reviewed it and smiled like a proud teacher.

My lack of sleep had me seeing things. For a moment, Cecil was looking good to me—in a nerdy sort of way. *I need a nap more than I need to study.* "Wake me up when the bell rings," I said.

Cecil responded, "No. You have homework to do so let's get to it."

I crossed my arms and leaned back in my chair. *Did he just tell me no?* I yawned and laid my head on the desk. "I'll call you tonight."

"I have a tournament I'm preparing for tonight so it's either now or tomorrow during study hall."

I sat up and pulled out my notebook and pencil. "Man, Cecil, you sound like my teacher."

He pulled his chair closer to mine and he walked me through a few of my problems. By the time I figured out how to do the problems by myself, it was time to go to the next class. I surprised Cecil and myself by giving him a hug before leaving.

I was still excited about my A when I met up with Britney and Sierra at lunch. They weren't as thrilled as I was, but I didn't care. "You're supposed to be proud of my accomplishments," I said as I boasted.

"We are, but that's all you've been talking about since you sat down," Sierra said.

"You don't hear me complaining about your dance team." Britney and Sierra both could dance better than me but I would never admit it to them. I couldn't wait until cheerleader tryouts. I planned on being a cheerleader my sophomore year.

"Hi, Jasmine," Cecil said as he walked by our table.

I waved at him. Britney and Sierra looked at me strangely. "What?"

"Last time he spoke to you in the cafeteria, you almost bit his head off," Britney noted.

I took a bite out of my hamburger. "That was then,

this is now," I responded. "Besides, he did help me get the A. The least I could do is say something to him when he speaks to me."

Britney and Sierra continued to exchange looks with one another. Sierra said, "I've been meaning to say something. I thought you were giving up meat."

I put my half-eaten hamburger down. "I said I was thinking about it. I'm still thinking."

Britney said, "I'm not giving up meat. I'll give up bread before I give up meat."

Sierra said, "I like bread and meat."

"We can tell," I responded.

Britney mouthed the words, *Don't go there.*

I shrugged my shoulders. It wasn't my fault that Sierra was getting a little chunky. I admit, she's not fat, but she had put on some weight since junior high school. I was only concerned about her weight for health reasons. Her weight was a sensitive subject so I dropped it.

Some guy who I hadn't noticed before stopped by our table. "Which one of you is Jasmine?" he asked.

Britney responded, "Why? Who are you?"

"I heard you had a mouth on you. I was wondering if we could maybe go out sometime."

"I don't think so," I responded.

"Oh, yeah, he did say it was the short one." He threw a piece a paper on the table. "If you change your mind, call me." He walked away from the table. DJ and his friends burst out laughing.

"He got his nerves." Sierra grabbed the piece of paper to look at it. "Jeffrey. He's a trip."

"I can't stand DJ," I said with clenched teeth.

"Me neither. Isn't he tired of trying to make our lives miserable?"

"He can try all he wants to but I refuse to be one of his victims."

"That's what I'm talking about," Britney said, giving me a high five. I figured she must have forgiven me for what I said about Sierra.

We emptied our trays and walked by DJ's table looking him square in the face. *If he thought he could break me down, he was sadly mistaken. I'm Jasmine McNeil and I don't bow down to nobody.*

Brenda picked me up after school. Sierra rode with Britney so it was just the two of us. I told her about what happened at lunch. "Just let the guys know you aren't to be messed with and they'll leave you alone," she said.

"Check this out. What if you thought you liked this guy but then found out that you didn't, but he keeps calling you anyway? How do you get him to stop calling you?"

"After I tell a man to stop calling me and he still does, I block his number," Brenda responded.

"I tried that. But he sends me instant messages every time I pop on the computer."

She held up her hand. "Block."

"I did that last night so hopefully that'll work."

My BlackBerry vibrated. *Unknown* was displayed in place of the caller ID. It was probably William, so I hit the ignore button. "That's him again. I swear. I'm tired of dealing with him."

"Jas, I can swing by the store and we can have them change your number now."

"I don't think so." I went on about Soulja Boy and my hopes of him calling me.

Brenda laughed and laughed. I didn't find it funny. I said, "You all just don't understand. I cannot change my number."

"Deal with it. Eventually, he'll get tired of calling."

"I hope so, because he's getting on my nerves."

We were near our home. Brenda said, "I need to warn you, Mom's not in the best of moods."

I hung my head down. "What did Dad do now?"

"One of her friends told her about a picture on the Internet so she's mad about that."

"I was hoping she wouldn't find out," I said.

"You knew about it and didn't tell me?" Brenda asked.

"Sort of. I was hoping it would just go away."

"Well, after overhearing mom go off on Dad over

the phone, I did a search on the Net and saw it. It said Mom and Dad were trying out for this reality show. I asked Mom if she wanted me to bring her something back from the store and she nearly bit my head off. At that point, I decided not to ask her anything about it."

I squirmed in my seat. *Should I or shouldn't I tell her?* "Bren, there's something I want to tell you, but you have to promise me you won't say anything to Mom or Dad."

"I can't do that."

"Then I'll keep the information to myself." I turned up the volume on the stereo.

Brenda turned it off. "Oh no you don't, missy. What's going on? You might as well tell me because I'll find out sooner or later."

My BlackBerry vibrated again. It was my phone alerting me to a voice mail. "That might be my tutor." *Whew, saved by the phone.*

19

Situation Number Nine

I called Cecil and acted like he had left me a message. He was practicing for his math-a-thon but took the time to talk to me. By that time, we were home, so I told Cecil I would speak to him later. Brenda was in a hurry to drop me off, so she didn't try to press me for more information about the info she read on the Internet. She waited for me to get in the house before speeding away.

"Mom, I'm home," I yelled out. The sound of my voice echoed. I looked in the rooms downstairs for her before going up to her bedroom. Just in case she was sleeping, I lightly tapped on her bedroom door. I didn't get a response. I turned the doorknob and peeked in the room. Sure enough, she was sleeping. There were many pieces of tissues laid around her.

She must have been crying. I slipped back out the room without waking her up.

I was digging through my book bag when my phone rang. I checked the caller ID first just in case it was William. A number I didn't recognize was displayed with the area code 310. I answered it. The person on the other end said, "This is Lily, a producer with the show *Situation Number Nine*. Is Kimberly or Dion McNeil available?"

Oh my goodness. I couldn't believe it. The reality show producer was actually calling me. Well, calling my mom. Should I wake her up and let her speak with them?

"Hello. Anybody there," Lily repeated herself.

I cleared my throat. "Yes, this is Kimberly," I said, in my best Mom impression.

"Good. There are a few questions I had about your application. First of all, I wanted to say, we were thrilled that you and your husband were interested in being on our show. You'll be our first celebrity or semi-celebrity couple."

"Cool." I would try to keep my responses to a few words, so I wouldn't slip up.

"A few of us wanted to fly down and meet you two in person; just to make sure this is something you really want to do. Would next week work out for you?"

I put the phone away from my mouth and paced the floor. *Next week!* Think. What do I tell her?

"Mrs. McNeil, is next week good for you?"

"Let me check with Dion and I'll call you back. Do you have a number I can reach you at?" I flipped through my notebook and found a blank page and wrote down her contact information.

"If next week doesn't work, maybe the week after. We need to know soon because we want to start filming as soon as possible," Lily commented.

"I'm just so excited. Let me talk to Dion and I'll call you back."

I threw the phone down and danced to celebrate. "We're going to be on TV."

"Girl, what are you keeping up all this noise for?" my mom walked in the room and asked, catching me doing my celebration dance.

I ran up to her and hugged her. "Good news. We are going to save your marriage."

She pulled away. "Jas, dear. I got this. You just worry about pulling up your grades."

"No, you don't understand. I've already set it up. Look."

"Jasmine, what have you done?"

'Nothing Mom, you'll see." I pulled her over to my desk. I logged onto the computer and went to *Situa-*

tion Number Nine's home page. She read it and turned and looked at me.

"What does this have to do with my marriage?"

"Mom. See, I got you and Dad on the show."

"When? How did this happen?"

"I filled out the application and sent it in and they called."

"You did what?"

I walked to my bed and tore the paper out of my notebook with the number and handed it to her. "The producer called today. They want you to call them back and let them know if they can come next week."

"Jas, I don't know what kind of mess you've gotten us in, but there is no way I will be going on anybody's reality show." My mom sounded upset at me.

It wasn't the type of response I had expected. I thought she would be more excited about it.

"But Mom, this is your chance to force Dad to get counseling."

"I can't force your dad to do anything. Besides, I don't want everybody and their mama all up in my business. I have a hard enough time dealing with these folks here in Dallas."

"But folks are already in your business. Stuff is showing up on the Internet," I reminded her.

"Right now, folks are speculating. They don't know what's true and what isn't. Let them talk. I refuse to give them things to talk about." She stood with her hand on her hip.

"But—" I stammered. Now I wasn't so sure the reality TV show was a good idea.

"No buts. Wait until I tell Dion about this. What am I going to do with you, girl?" She rushed out of the room.

I plopped down on my bed. I couldn't give up. I had to keep my folks together.

I called Britney and Sierra on the three-way. "What am I going to do? They're not going to make it unless they get some counseling."

"Calm down, Jas. Give your mom some time to think it over. She might change her mind," Britney said.

"I doubt it." I had no hope that she would change her mind.

Sierra said, "Why don't you try to make her feel guilty? Go tell her that she needs to do it for you. If she does it and their marriage doesn't work out, at least you'll know she did all she could."

Hmm. That might work. "Sierra, you're a genius."

"That's what they tell me." She laughed.

"I'll talk to y'all later because Operation Keep My Parents Together has gone to the next level."

I hung up with them and rushed to locate my mom. She was combing through her hair. I took the comb from her and combed her hair like I used to do when I was a little girl. She had thick black hair and I used to love to comb through it. "Mama, I know you don't want to do it but if you don't do it, how will you know you did everything you could to make it work?"

She didn't respond; instead she took the comb away from me and placed her hair in a ponytail. She got up and I followed her to the chaise located near her bedroom window. She looked out the window while talking. "I've given Dion twenty-one years of my life. When I met him, he was playing for Texas A and M. The girls were all crazy about him, but your dad seemed to only have eyes for me."

She had a faraway look in her eyes. She continued her story. "I knew he slept with other girls sometimes, but I didn't care because I loved me some Dion. Besides, we weren't married and I figured he should get it out of his system because once he was married, I would be the only woman he would know in that way."

"So you slept with Dad before y'all got married?"

"Dear, what your dad and I did before you got here is our business."

"But, you told me that it's best to wait until you're married before having sex."

"And I still feel that way. You're not having sex, are you?"

"Uh, no, Mom. That's not even on my mind."

"I'm just checking, because some of you little girls are hot to trot."

I listened to her go on about the importance of practicing abstinence. I had to steer this conversation back to her and Dad doing the reality show. Talking about sex with my mom was a little too uncomfortable. Besides, I wasn't thinking about having sex with anyone until I was either in college or married. Seeing what happened to Tanisha last semester was enough drama for me. I didn't want to risk getting pregnant like her and having to drop out of school, nor did I want to get a disease that could kill me. I loved myself too much to let that happen.

"It's obvious you and Dad still love each other," I said.

She reached out for my hand. Her eyes watered. "When you're together as long as we have, the love gets comfortable. I think that's the place we're at now. He wants more than I can give him, I'm afraid."

"I promise if you try this one thing and it doesn't work, I won't pressure you or him again. I've watched the show and I've seen couples get back together."

"I've told you about watching all of that stuff on that station."

"I know, Mom, but there's nothing else on TV so I have to watch the reality shows."

"My little girl is growing up. Here you are trying to give me advice on my marriage, when I should be talking to you about boys. Speaking of boys, anybody interesting this semester? What was that other boy's name you said was giving you a quote-"headache"-unquote last semester?"

"DJ and he's still a pain in the—" I paused before continuing. "You know what."

"Watch your mouth now. You're not grown yet."

I got closer to my mom and hugged her. "So will you do the show? Do it for me, please." I batted my eyes and pouted.

"I'll think about it."

"Yes," I yelled. I squeezed her tight.

"Don't go celebrating yet. I still have to run this past Dion."

"Don't worry, Mom. Leave Dad to me."

20

Daddy's Girl

My mom and I plotted together. We had to convince my dad to do the show. She cooked dinner and I went to my room to finish my homework. Hopefully, he wouldn't be late getting home tonight so we could work on him. I was excited. "My mom's going to do it," I said as I talked to Britney on the phone.

"I don't know how you do it, but girl, you can convince anybody to do anything you want."

"Skills that I get from my dad, so I hope they'll work on him."

"Keep making them feel guilty. It worked on your mom," Britney suggested.

"He's here now. My mom just called me down for

dinner. I'll call you later and let you know how it went."

I rushed downstairs. I gave my dad a great big hug and kiss on the cheek and took my seat around the table. Brenda rolled her eyes at me. I didn't care. Not even Brenda was going to deter me from my goals. The conversation over dinner was light. I laughed at my dad's jokes even when they weren't funny. I kept looking at my mom to see when I should ask him about the show, but she never would look at me. I hoped she hadn't changed her mind.

After dinner, my mom made Brenda do the dishes so it left me alone with my dad. I followed him to the den. He turned the TV to his favorite sports station. I would have to work fast because if a game was coming on, I would not get his attention. Fortunately, it was just commercials.

"Daddy, remember you said I could always count on you?" I batted my eyes for extra measure.

"What do you need, Jasmine?" He reached into his wallet and pulled out a few hundred dollar bills.

"I don't need any money, but I'll take it." I reached for the money, but he pulled his hand away.

"Then what is it?"

"I see things are better between you and Mama and I just wanted to say thank you."

"We're trying, but I can't make you any promises that we'll stay together."

"But that's just it. I'm happy that you're trying. It means a lot to me."

He smiled. "Good. I just want my little half-pint to be happy."

"*Dadddd.*" I let the *d* drag out, showing my irritation. He knew I hated for him to call me half-pint. As far as he was concerned, I would always be his little half-pint.

Some sports commentator came on the air. I would have to wait for a commercial to come on or else he wouldn't hear me. I tried to go over in my head what I would say. When the show went on commercial break, I just blurted it out. "I signed you and Mom up for *Situation Number Nine* and they'll be here next week." *Whew. I did it.*

I stood up to leave. He patted on the couch and said in a calm voice, "Jasmine, sit your butt right back down."

I did as I was told. He shouted, "Kim, come here."

My mom looked at me. I looked down at the floor. "Why are you yelling?"

"Do you know about this *Situation Number Nine* show this child is talking about?"

"She told me about it earlier. Do you want to do it or not?"

"You got to be kidding. I'm trying to get this commentator gig on ESPN and you're talking about a reality show."

"It'll make ESPN take notice. You'll be sure to get the job then," she insisted.

"I have four Super Bowl rings. I don't need a reality show for them to notice me."

"Dad, please. Do it for me. *Pleasssse*," I interrupted.

"Dion, think about it. You like all the attention. We can get free counseling and satisfy your daughter at the same time."

"No wonder our child's a drama queen."

"She gets it from you, but you can't see that."

"Kim, I don't feel like arguing with you. Can't we just get along one day without bickering?"

Oh no. It's the Dion and Kim show. And he doesn't want to do a reality show. Watching them two would be entertaining if they weren't my parents. I crossed my legs under each other and watched them go back and forth. I picked up the remote and flipped stations until they got tired of arguing. My dad took the remote from me and turned it back to *Sports-Center*.

"Jasmine, I suggest you go to bed so you won't oversleep." He didn't want a response, because he turned the volume up without waiting for one.

My mom motioned for me to leave. I obeyed without giving them flack. I left the room without looking back. Brenda was sitting at the bottom of the stairway. "So you're the one who leaked the information to the gossip blog?"

"No, it wasn't me." I rolled my eyes at her. I bumped her as I walked up the stairs. She was fast on my heels.

"You are always up to something. You couldn't stay out of it. Now they might really get a divorce because of you," she yelled.

"I thought you wanted them to break up. You were looking for divorce attorneys for Mom and everything," I responded.

"Silly girl," she said, before storming away.

This time I ran behind her. We ended up in her room. "I was trying to help. I didn't know it would cause them to fight."

Brenda turned around to face me. Her face had softened, which eased some of the tension between us. "I'm sorry, okay. I didn't mean to yell at you. Being here is like a war zone. I'm really thinking about moving out to my own place."

My whole family was being torn apart. Brenda couldn't leave me. "Bren, I can't be here by myself. Mom is so wrapped up with Dad. Dad's hardly here. Who am I going to have around to argue with?"

Brenda laughed. We both fell on her bed. "I'm not going anywhere unless Dad's footing the bill and the way he's been tight on money lately, I doubt he would pay my rent."

I felt relieved. Brenda and I argued all of the time but I loved my sister just as much as I loved my parents. I didn't want to imagine life without her here to give me grief. "Do you think they'll do it?"

"I say wait and see. If they do, it'll surprise me." She turned the TV on and we watched an episode of *America's Next Top Model.*

I fell asleep. I felt a gentle nudge. Brenda's bed was comfortable. I didn't feel like getting up. She threw a blanket over me and fell asleep on the other side of the bed.

"I was wondering where you were," my mom said the next morning as she entered Brenda's room.

"We had a bonding session," Brenda teased.

I threw a pillow at her as I sat up. "Can I call in sick today?" I asked.

"Nope, so I suggest you go get ready," my mom responded.

I dragged myself to my room and I didn't completely perk up until the hot water hit me in the shower. By the time I was dressed for school, my mom had breakfast waiting for us. For the first time, in a long time, Brenda and I didn't argue when she drove me to school. Operation Rescue My Parents looked like it was a bust. I had no plan C.

21

Homeroom

I chatted with Britney and Sierra about my latest drama at home while we walked to our first class. Mrs. Johnson wasn't in class again this morning. I wondered what kind of accident she had because it was unlike her to be absent. We talked until the substitute teacher from the day before entered into the room.

Some of the girls in the class seemed to be under his spell, but not me. There was something about him that I didn't like. He seemed to call on me for every little thing. He was becoming a nuisance. I stared at him as he lectured the class from his notes. I didn't bother to write anything down. I would get a copy of Sierra's notes later.

"Jasmine McNeil, can I see you after class?"

What is it with this teacher? "Go ahead. I'll catch y'all later," I said to Britney and Sierra.

I stood by the desk. Apparently, he was waiting for the class to clear, because he didn't acknowledge me until after everyone was out of the room. He stood up as if he was going to close the door. I rushed to the door to block him from doing so.

"Wait," he said, as he reached out to touch my shoulder.

I jerked my arm back. "The bell has rung, so can you please tell me what you want so I won't be late." I was trying my best not to be disrespectful to my elder, although he looked like he was more of Brenda's age than Mrs. Johnson's.

"I'll write you a pass."

"No, thank you." He was really making me feel uncomfortable. I rushed past him and didn't wait for him to say anything else.

While in class, I wrote a note to Sierra and Britney asking them to make sure they were not late for lunch because something strange was going on. I handed them each a note in between classes.

I avoided eye contact with DJ and his friends while in the hallway outside the lunchroom. Sierra and Britney both were waiting for me outside. "Is it DJ again?" Britney asked.

"I'll tell you when we sit down." I looked over my

shoulder. DJ and crew were behind us in line making noises. The cafeteria monitor told them to quiet it down.

I barely ate my food as I told them about the strange encounter with our substitute homeroom teacher. "He sort of reminds me of William. He sounded like him when he was up there lecturing."

"He can't be. You said William is a senior at Roosevelt. Mr. White looks like he's twentysomething at least," Britney noted.

"Answer this. Why was he about to close the door?" I asked.

Neither Britney nor Sierra could answer that question. Sierra said, "Maybe we should report it to the principal. If he's a pervert or something, they need to know."

"But what if it's just Jasmine's imagination. The man could lose his job," Britney said.

"Let's hope Mrs. Johnson will be back tomorrow because I have enough drama going on at home. I don't need to deal with it here at school too."

"Speaking of Mrs. Johnson—don't look now, but there's the substitute teacher," Sierra said.

"And he's headed straight to our table," Britney said.

"Hi, ladies. You don't mind if I sit with you, do you?" he asked.

I looked at Britney and Sierra to say something, but they didn't, so I said, "We were just about to leave, so you can have this table."

He looked at his watch. "You still have a ten more minutes before your next class."

I placed my uneaten food and half-empty juice container on my tray. *They could sit and talk to him, if they wanted to, but not me. I'm out of here.* I stood up and left the table and fortunately, they followed me.

We walked out the cafeteria. Britney said, "That was too weird. I see what you mean."

"He made my flesh crawl," I said. My phone vibrated. It was a text message. I almost dropped my phone. I leaned into Sierra. She almost lost her balance as she tried to hold me up.

"Girl, you all right?" Sierra asked.

I handed her the phone. Britney and Sierra read the message. "I don't recall having a butterfly logo on the picture I posted online," I stated.

"Did you wear it Saturday? Maybe that's when he saw it," Sierra suggested.

"Even if she did, he wasn't close enough to see her. They only saw each other in passing, remember," Britney said.

"Are you going to respond to him?" Sierra asked.

"No. Now that I know he has a new e-mail address,

I will block it too." I blocked William's new address while we walked down the hall.

They walked me to my class and we stayed outside and talked until the bell rang. After school, Brenda waited in her normal spot; however, she was standing beside her car talking to Mr. White. Brenda waved her hand to get my attention. I waved back to let her know I saw her. My pace decreased as I walked in her direction.

"Is the door unlocked?" I asked.

Brenda hit a button on the remote and the alarm beeped twice. I threw my backpack in the backseat and sat in the front. She was taking too long so I reached and rolled down her window. "Hey, hurry up; I have to go to the bathroom."

She asked, "Why didn't you go before you came out?"

"Because I didn't have to go then, but now I do," I responded.

I couldn't hear what she said to Mr. White. She got in the car. I looked in his direction. He waved at me. I didn't wave back. "How do you know him?" I asked as Brenda pulled away.

"I met him last year. We had a few classes together."

"Did y'all ever go out?"

"Oh but no. He's not my type. He's too needy for me."

"How do you know that if you never went out with him?"

"I knew someone who did. She told me all I needed to know."

"I was just checking. He's been substituting for Mrs. Johnson. I don't like him."

"Oh, he must be making you do some work. I've heard your friends say you're Mrs. Johnson's favorite."

"That has nothing to do with it. It's just something about him that I don't like."

"I wouldn't worry about it if I were you. He said Mrs. Johnson was supposed to be back tomorrow. So see, you can go back to being the teacher's pet." She laughed.

Just when Brenda and I were making some progress in the sister department, she was back to getting on my nerves. I guess things were back to normal again.

22

My Lip Gloss is Cool

"If you put on any more lip gloss, the planes will be able to see how to land," Mrs. Johnson said before I got up to leave homeroom.

"I missed you too, Mrs. Johnson," I said, smiling.

"Well, you better hurry up out of here because I'm not writing you a pass for your next class."

"Did you have the flu or something?" I asked her.

"No, it was food poisoning. I hadn't been that sick a day in my life. Thanks for your concern. Now, child, go on now so you won't be late."

The rest of the week went by in a breeze. Things were quiet at home because my parents were on two different schedules. My dad left early in the morning and got home late at night. My mom avoided long conversations with me and that was all right with me because when she was talking to me, she was snapping at me. She probably blamed me like Brenda did for causing the argument the other night. I hoped she could forgive me.

It was Friday and I wished I was hanging out with Britney or Sierra but instead I was sitting home bored. I logged on to the computer to check my My-Space page. Some of my friends were on, so I chatted with them for awhile. It had been less than a week and I was totally over my William withdrawal. I was about to log off MySpace until I got a message from Cecil. I should have known he was home on a Friday night. That wasn't nice of me. Cecil looks all right and he would be cool if he would get rid of those nerdy-looking glasses.

NumbersIsMe: U need 2 change your music.

DFWCutie: Don't visit my page if U don't like it.

NumbersIsMe: I didn't say I didn't like it. The song is old.

DFWCutie: I love lip gloss. Perfect song 4 me. Sing along with me . . . "My lip gloss is cool . . ."

NumbersIsMe: LOL. Jas U got jokes.

I laughed at the thought of Cecil singing Lil Mama's song. We chatted for over an hour and then he decided to get off. Still bored, I logged into one of the chat rooms. Big mistake, because TallandFly was in the chat room. I logged off real quick. Shortly thereafter, I got an instant message from someone I wasn't familiar with. Curiosity got the best of me, so I accepted it.

BlueMagic: Hey Cutie.
DFWCutie: Hi Magic.
BlueMagic: How old are you?
DFWCutie: 16. U?
BlueMagic: 24.

I had never talked to an older guy.

DFWCutie: U probably think I'm 2 young.
BlueMagic: 16's not 2 young. It's just right.

"Girl, you better get off the computer talking to older guys," Brenda said over my shoulder.

I didn't even hear her come in.

"Move," she said, as she took over my typing.

DFWCutie: This is Cutie's older sister. Unless
             U want me 2 report U 2 the police,
             U will not contact her again.

BlueMagic logged off seconds later.

Brenda said, "Girl, didn't I tell you about being careful on the Internet."

"He was only twenty-four. It's not like he was the same age as my biology teacher."

"Twenty-four is too old for you. Trust me. If he's older than sixteen, you shouldn't be dealing with him."

I had to listen to Brenda lecture me on Internet safety. I had heard the speech before. *Never give out your name or address. Don't talk to older guys.*

"Just never give out personal information, period. Understood?" she said at the end of her lecture.

"I've only talked to one guy off the Net." I didn't mean to let that slip. Since I did, I went on to tell her about him and the incident at the mall.

"Now it explains why you were asking all of those questions. You better hope Mom don't find out about it."

"I don't talk to him anymore so there's no need for her to know," I said.

"At least you were smart enough to stop talking to him. Promise me you won't ever do it again."

I crossed my fingers on the hand that was held behind my back and said, "Promise."

"I'll play you in a game of Monopoly," she said.

We stayed up until after midnight playing the game

on the computer. My parents went from arguing all of the time to barely saying anything to one another. Imagine my surprise on Monday morning, when my dad said, "Half-pint, my agent wants me to do the show. He thinks it'll be good for my image."

Yes. "Thank you, Daddy." I hugged him and ran to get in Brenda's car.

"What took you so long?" she asked.

"Dad's going to do the show."

"I can't believe it," she responded, as she pulled out the driveway.

"We're going to be on TV," I sang over and over.

"Brat, you might keep them together after all."

"I hope so," I responded as I rolled the watermelon lip gloss over my lips.

23

Baby, I'm a Star

"I don't know if I would want my whole life taped," Sierra said while we talked over lunch.

"It would be kind of boring to watch you do nothing," I teased. Even Britney had to laugh, because Sierra was the most boring person out of the three of us.

"See, that's why I need to get me a new set of friends. Because y'all two don't appreciate me." She sniffed a few times.

"Oh my goodness. Look who's the drama queen now," I said.

Sierra said, "Jas, you still got dabs on that."

I ignored her as I took out my compact mirror and refreshed my lip gloss. I bumped into Cecil on my way to class. I didn't immediately recognize him because he didn't have on his glasses. "Looking good, CC," I said, and kept on walking. I was right. Without the glasses, Cecil looked like a totally different guy.

My week seemed to go in slow motion as I waited for the day the producers from the show would show up. Wednesday after school, my mom treated me and Brenda to an afternoon spa. We got the works. All of us had our hair, nails, and facials. It was after eight before we got home. My dad wasn't too happy to come home to an empty house. I later found out he was more upset that my mom had hired someone to clean the house.

"Kim, we're trying to save money, but you keep spending money."

"I can't have people coming over here and the house not be clean. You know that's unacceptable."

"You've been doing a good job cleaning. Why did you have to go pay for a maid?"

"They can get in places I just can't get to." What my dad didn't know is my mom had no intentions of getting rid of a maid completely. She said we could still afford a maid once a week so unless something drastic happened, she would continue to use one. My dad just happened to find out about it. I hoped they kissed and made up before the producers came tomorrow.

"Are the people at the house?" I asked Brenda the next day after school as she was driving me home.

"I haven't been home yet. I'm a little nervous about meeting them."

"Me too. They have to pick us, though. We're like the American family."

"I wouldn't say all of that."

When we pulled up to our house, the driveway was filled with two black SUVs that didn't belong to us. Brenda and I both checked our appearances in the mirror before exiting her car. I grabbed my backpack and Brenda grabbed her purse. I followed her to the door. She did as we rehearsed in preparation for the cameras. She pretended to have forgotten her keys, so Mom would have an excuse to come to the door.

"Girls, you made it," my mom said as she opened the door, wearing a cream-colored pantssuit and a cameraman standing right behind her filming.

Brenda said, "I forgot my key."

"That's okay, dear. Ladies, we have company. Why don't you put your stuff down over there so I can introduce you."

"Lily, these are my daughters, Brenda and Jasmine," she said to a tall, slender woman wearing a fuchsia suit.

We shook hands. My dad was entertaining two other people, a woman who was a few inches taller than me and an older man. I didn't immediately see the camera. Lily said, "Don't mind him. He's just getting some footage for us to look at later."

A smile flashed across my face as I followed behind them and sat on the couch. Lily asked, "Jasmine, what are some things you like to do?"

"I like to hang out with my friends . . . shop . . . talk on the phone . . . surf the Internet . . . just normal stuff."

"How do you feel about your parents doing the show?"

"I think it's great."

"Would you have a problem if we followed you around at school one day?"

Before I could answer, my father intervened. "Her school's off-limits. You can talk to her before and after, but we don't want her normal routine interrupted during her schooltime."

My mom added, "We would prefer if you limited the taping of our kids to the confinement of the house."

Lily wrote down something on her notepad. She asked Brenda a few questions and then we were dismissed. I asked Brenda as we were walking up the stairs, "How did I do?"

"You tried to hog all the camera time, but that's cool."

"I can't help it because I'm the cute one," I responded.

"You wish," she said as she went to her room and I went to mine.

I called Britney and Sierra and told them about my experience in front of the camera. I couldn't wait to find out if they were going to choose my parents to be on the show. I logged on to the Internet and surfed all the gossip blogs. There wasn't anything new on there about my dad, so that was good news.

I fantasized that Soulja Boy would be contacting me once he saw me on the show. My mom entered my room interrupted my fantasy. "You can come back downstairs now. They're gone."

"What's for dinner?" I asked.

"Your dad's going to pick up something from Tony Roma's, so he'll be back in about an hour."

"Can you fix me something real quick? I'm hungry now," I said, rubbing my stomach.

"Baby, you're not a star yet. You can wait until he gets back."

24

Somebody Help Me Please

The next week we found out my parents were chosen for the show. I hated that I couldn't tell anybody at school about it, but at least I could tell my friends. Britney and Sierra both planned to stop by during one night of taping. "You know what this means?" I said.

Together we said, "Shopping."

"Y'all need to hold it down over there," the librarian said.

We lowered our voices and continued to make shopping plans. Brenda took us to the mall after school and we all picked out some color-coordinated clothes. "My dad's going to kill me when or if he finds out I charged something else," Sierra said.

"I could have paid for it and you could have just

given me the money when you got your allowance," Bridget said.

"Oh well. Being on a national TV show will make getting in trouble worth it."

"My mom says your parents will have to sign off on a release form so they can film you."

"Then I might not be able to do it. You know how my dad is. He would love to ruin this for me," Sierra said, pouting.

"I'll have my mom ask your mom," I said.

"That'll be better."

Britney said, "I'm sure my parents won't have a problem with it."

Britney flipped open her phone. "Marcus, let me call you back." She hung the phone up and said, "He is getting on my nerves."

"Why do you still talk to him then?" I asked.

Sierra answered for her, "Because she still likes him."

"Maybe. I mean, we're friends, but I don't like him in any other kind of way."

"What happened to that other dude? The one from your church?" Sierra asked.

"Travis is cool. He asked me to his Valentine's dance."

"What—and you're just telling us about it," I said.

"It's no big deal." Britney shrugged her shoulders.

"You're the only one of us who has a date for the Valentine's dance," I said.

"I don't know if I'm going because I'm waiting to see what my dad says."

"He let you go with Marcus," Sierra said.

"I know, but that was different. That was to our school dance. Travis goes to Mesquite High, which is on the other side of town."

"Why don't we all go? Travis can introduce us to some of his friends," I suggested.

"You know what, that'll work. That way my dad will have no choice but to let me go."

We went to find us semiformal dresses to wear to the dance since the date was right around the corner.

Brenda called to let me know she was ready. When we got to the car, she said, "Dang, y'all bought out the whole store. I hope I have room in my trunk for all of that."

"Don't squash my dress," I said.

"Just give me your stuff. I know what I'm doing. I'm dropping off Sierra first, so I need her stuff last."

Fifteen minutes later, we were on the freeway. An hour later we pulled up in front of our house. Brenda helped me carry my bags to my room. "This is a cute dress. If I didn't have these hips, I would wear it,"

Brenda said as she placed the knee-length red dress in front of her and admired herself in the mirror. "You know what. The way this material is, it might work."

I grabbed it from her. "I don't think so. You better get your own."

"What else you got here?" She went through some of my other bags. She found my new tube of grape delight lip gloss. "This smells good. Do you have an extra tube?"

"Sure, you can have that one. I just bought it in case I run out."

"You sure? I know how you are when it comes to your lip gloss."

"Take it before I change my mind."

Brenda put the top back on it and slipped it in her pocket. "Y'all did on the clothes. I didn't find me anything. I'll probably go to the Galleria tomorrow."

"I want to go."

"By the time you get out of school, I'll be through shopping."

"Can you buy me a bottle of that perfume you wouldn't let me have?"

"Sure. Their gift sets are out so I'll get you the whole set."

I hugged her. "You're the best sister ever."

She playfully pushed me out of the way. "Yes, you

say that now. If you have some homework, you better get to it. It's pizza night for us two. The folks are out again."

"I'm happy they're getting out more and doing things together."

"I'll keep my comments to myself," Brenda said.

"Is there something I should know that you're not telling me?" I asked.

"Enjoy your life. You're too young to be worried about grown folks' business." Brenda pulled her cell phone out of her pocket and ordered pizza. "I'll be downstairs. I'll let you know when the pizza comes."

I did my easy homework first. Before I could get started on my algebra, Brenda yelled the pizza was downstairs. "I'll eat mine upstairs, because I want to knock out this math." I threw a few slices on a disposable plate and grabbed a drink out of the refrigerator.

I ended up waiting to do my math until after I ate, because the formulas and pepperoni didn't mix well. "Cecil, help," I screamed from my end of the phone.

"I got the same book you have, so tell me the page and we can walk through it together."

That's what I liked about Cecil. He was always there when I called him. After an hour, Cecil had walked me through my homework. There was an awkward silence on the phone. "Thanks for coming to my rescue—again."

25

Love Is In the Air

All of our parents agreed to let us go to Mesquite High's Valentine's Dance. Sierra and I got dressed at Britney's. We all looked good in our chosen attire. I had on my knee-length red chiffon dress with a shawl, just in case the Texas night air was crisp. Britney wore a black and red strapless dress that made her look taller than she actually was. Sierra looked good in her black satin knee-length dress. Britney's mom wobbled into the room and insisted on taking our pictures. "I can't make it down the stairs, so we'll take it in here. My girls are growing up."

"Don't cry," Britney said. She looked at us. "She cries about everything now."

Once Britney and her mom were outside of the room, I told Sierra, "If getting pregnant would make

me look like Mrs. Franklin, I would never have babies. I don't think my body would ever look the same
after having a baby."

"I heard that," Mrs. Franklin said as she followed
Britney back in the room. "Dear, I better not hear
about you having sex until you're old and gray."

"Mom," Britney said, sounding embarrassed.

"I mean it. You girls try to grow up too fast. Hold
on to your youth as long as you can. It's no picnic
being a grown-up. Being grown-up comes with responsibilities. Right now, the only thing you three
have to worry yourselves with is making sure you
keep your grades up."

Here we go again. Not another lecture. She didn't
have to worry about me or Britney. Now Sierra; she
can be a little gullible about things, but after that fiasco with DJ, I think she learned a thing or two.

Mrs. Franklin stopped talking long enough for us
to take more pictures and head out the door. I was
thrilled that we would be riding in the Rolls-Royce.
Donovan, Britney's driver, probably wasn't happy
about escorting a bunch of teenage girls to and from
a dance, but we sure were happy that he was.

We listened to some of our favorite music on the
drive over. "I hope Travis has some cute friends,"
Sierra said as Donovan pulled up in front of Mesquite
High School.

"Me too," I said.

Several people watched us as we exited the car. We knew we were looking good. The girls rolled their eyes and the guys couldn't stop looking. We walked into their school's auditorium, like we were all that and then some. Everything looked pretty. There were red and white balloons everywhere. I was glad there was a DJ instead of a live band. I hated school dances where there were live bands.

"Travis better not stand me up," Britney said.

I pointed toward another door. "You don't have to worry about that. Here he comes now."

Sierra said, "Girl, he is fine. He looks way better than Marcus."

"He looks all right," Britney responded.

I'm sure she was smiling inside, because even I had to admit Travis looked good in his suit. I don't recall him looking this good at church. I hoped the boys walking with him were his friends because they were sort of cute too.

"Hi Britney," Travis said, giving her a hug. "Hi Jasmine."

He smelled good too.

Britney said, "This is Sierra, my other best friend I told you about."

They shook hands. Travis said, "This is Benjamin and Carlos. Y'all want something to drink."

After they left to get us something to drink, I said, "Sierra, which one do you like and I'll go for the other one."

"It doesn't matter. They both are cute."

Britney intervened. "Yes, it does matter. Tell her now because we don't want another DJ situation."

Sierra thought about it for a few seconds. "I'll take Carlos. I love his thick eyebrows."

We sealed it with a handshake. "Here they come," I said, trying to look cool.

It seemed that the fellows had talked too because Benjamin was the one who handed me my drink. It was good to see we were all on the same page. We paired off and went to the dance floor. In between dancing, we took pictures with the guys and by ourselves. Britney said, "It's eleven so I better get going because our curfew is midnight."

"One last dance," Travis said, holding out his hand to her.

"Hold these," she said, as she handed me her pictures and small clutch handbag.

"I guess I'm stuck holding these." Benjamin stayed by my side.

"Can I have your number so I maybe can call you sometime?" he asked.

I was hoping he asked me. If he hadn't asked for my number, I would have been disappointed. I know

I come across as confident when it comes to boys, but a part of me is shy and with boys you can never tell if they really like you or not. I typed my number into his cell phone and he locked it in. "I'll get your number when you call me," I said.

"I really had a good time. Travis has been trying to get me to come to church with him. He won't have to ask me again if you're going to be there."

"I'm usually at the eleven o'clock service. You'll see me. I'll be the cute one with the pretty eyes."

We both laughed. Britney, Travis, Sierra, and Carlos walked over to where we were standing. The guys walked us out to the car. We all hugged and Donovan had us back on LBJ Freeway before we knew it. He asked, "Did you ladies have a good time?"

"It was fun. I'm glad we went," Britney said.

"Okay. Well, I'll have you home soon. I'll let the window up so you can talk about the fun y'all had in private." I heard the window close.

"Travis kissed me," Britney said.

"How was it?" Sierra asked.

"I think I'm in love," she responded, and leaned back in her seat holding her heart.

"Was he better than Marcus?" I asked.

"Ten times better."

Uh-oh. Marcus really was history.

"I sort of like Benjamin too. What do you know about him?" I asked.

"He lives in Mesquite. He is a sophomore and he and Travis are friends. That's all I know."

"Girl, call Travis. I need the four-one-one . . . brothers . . . sisters . . . daddy . . . mama . . . the works."

"No. I'm not going to get in the middle of it."

"You have to. He's your man's friend."

"Travis is not my man."

"Yet," Sierra added.

Britney ignored her and continued to talk. "If Benjamin ends up being a jerk, I don't want to hear about it."

"You want," I said. "I just need to make sure he's not another DJ. You can easily find that out by asking Travis a few questions."

"Okay. I'll do it tomorrow." Britney asked Sierra. "Do you want me to find out about Carlos too?"

"Nope. Tonight will probably be the last time I see him."

"What happened? It looked like y'all were getting along," I said.

"We were, but he's not my type."

"Girl, you're not old enough to have a type," Britney said.

"He reminded me too much of DJ and I've learned my lesson."

"Did he try to force himself on you?" I asked.

"No, it wasn't that. He was nice and all, but he did try to catch a feel or two when we were slow dancing."

"You should have said something. I would have mentioned it to Travis," Britney said.

"It was no big deal. I handled it. He understood where I was coming from and he didn't try it again."

"I'm still saying something to Travis."

"Yes, you should," I said.

Britney dialed Travis's number and put him on speaker. "Your boy Carlos was trying to feel up my girl."

Travis apologized. "I'm sorry. I'll talk to him about it."

Sierra said, "You don't have to."

"Yes, you do," Britney said.

"Hold on a minute," he said.

He must have pressed the mute button because we couldn't hear anything on his end. "Sierra, you there?"

"Yes, who is this?"

"This is Carlos. I wanted to apologize again. I didn't mean any disrespect." He said a few words in Spanish.

Sierra responded in Spanish and then English. "We're cool. I'm just not that type of girl."

"Can I call you sometime?" he asked.

Sierra responded, "Let's just keep it like it is. When we see each other; which I'm sure we will since we have mutual friends, we'll hang out."

"It's your world. I'll see you when I see you."

Travis got back on the phone. "Everything cool now."

Britney took him off speakerphone. Sierra and I talked about her while she tried to quiet us down.

We started singing an old childhood song, "Britney and Travis sitting in the tree. K-i-s-s-i-n-g."

She tried to make us stop, but we were having too much fun mocking her.

26

Showtime

The following week, the reality TV show producers and their crew embarked on our house as if we were a private studio. All of the excitement from the night before had me late for school the next day. I called Britney and Sierra the night before to make sure they packed for an overnight stay since this would be the night we got filmed together. I couldn't be on national TV and not get my friends in the limelight too.

"Do I look okay?" Sierra asked as she fluffed out the curls in her hair.

"You look great, now move out the way so I can put on my lip gloss," Britney said as they fought over the mirror.

"I'm going downstairs now, so act natural. Get on the computer . . . read a magazine."

I checked my appearance one last time. Since coming from school, I had changed into a pair of House of Dereon jeans and cute Baby Phat shirt. I was wearing some brown mules with a low heel.

Lily and her crew were waiting for me downstairs. "There she is," she said, rushing over and adjusting my blouse, although it didn't need any adjustment. She said, "We'll get a few shots with you down here and then we'll follow you upstairs to meet your friends."

I was a little starstruck because Nicholas—no last name needed—was hosting the show. He was one of my favorite actors and here he was in our house. I sat on the couch opposite him as he asked me a few questions.

"Your dad might be retired from the NFL but he still has a lot of fans. Has his notoriety affected you in any way?"

"Not really. Hardly anyone at the school knows I'm his daughter."

"Doesn't that bother you?" Nicholas asked.

"No. I'm proud to be his daughter, but I like being anonymous."

"I'm sure the audience wants to know, are you a daddy's girl?"

I batted my eyes and pretended to blush. "Of course." I smiled into the camera.

"Has your parents' bickering affected you in any way?" he asked.

I was told to pretend like the cameras weren't there, but that was hard to do when the light was beaming in my face. "They don't fight that much," I lied.

"We've been here a few days and have seen a few shouting matches."

"Normally, they get along. I'm glad they decided to try to get some help, though."

"Your mom told us you were instrumental in getting them on the show. How did you convince them to do *Situation Number Nine*?"

"It was easy. They both care about each other and about us as a family. They were willing to do whatever it takes to keep us together."

"Even if that means exposing themselves to the public . . . all of America . . . this is what this show is all about."

At that point, the cameras were cut off.

"Take five and then we'll be ready to follow you upstairs," Lily said.

I was hoping to get a chance to talk more with Nicholas, but he made a quick exit to the other side of the room to use his phone. While waiting, I pulled out some lip gloss and reapplied some to my lips. Once I made sure my lips were popping, I took a seat and waited for my cue. Shortly, Lily came back to where I was sitting and said, "The cameras are on. Talk to the cameras like you're giving a friend a private tour of your room. Just like on *MTV Cribs*."

That's all she had to say. I would give them the grand tour. I was in front of the camera. "This is where I do my homework," I said as I opened my bedroom door. I made sure my autographed Soulja Boy poster was in full display. "As you can tell, I love Soulja Boy." I walked over so the camera could get me standing next to one of my posters.

"These are my best friends in the whole wide world—Britney and Sierra." Sierra was seated at my computer desk, on the Internet, and Britney was sitting on the edge of the bed reading a fashion magazine.

They both looked into the camera and waved.

I went over to my vanity area and said, "This is where I keep all my tubes of lip gloss. As you can tell, I love lip gloss." The cameraman zoomed in on the various tubes, styles, and flavors of my lip gloss collection.

"Besides lip gloss, I love clothes. My closet is small compared to my mom's but it'll do." I walked over and opened up my walk-in closet. My clothes were all in their proper places. I had a section for my everyday wear, my uniforms for special occasions, a rack for my shoes, and a special case for my purses. "I know it seems like a lot, but I wear everything in it. We clear out our closets at least once a year. What I don't wear, even if it has a tag still on it, I have to give to a shelter."

I didn't want folks to think that I just had a whole bunch of stuff and didn't do anything. I wasn't lying about the shelter. My mom made us donate stuff we didn't wear after a year. Her rule was fine with me, because that meant I could get new stuff.

I sat down on the bed next to Britney. I said, "It's Friday night and we usually have a sleepover once a month. It's my month to host, so I get to decide what we'll do."

Britney said, "We're supposed to decide together."

Sierra added, "But Jas likes to have things her way, so this is the one time we let her."

I rolled my eyes at her and said, "Anyway." I took the magazine from Britney and put it on the bed. I stood up. "I have some new movies—so America, I guess we'll be watching movies tonight."

The cameraman stopped filming and said, "You girls continue to do what you do. I'll get you setting up the movie, but we'll take a break until after the movie is over and then start back filming."

Apparently, the cameraman forgot what he had told me earlier, because he was still filming us as we talked about our favorite subjects—boys. Britney wasn't sure if she wanted to be Travis's girlfriend.

"My mom says I'm too young, but I really do like Travis. I can't forget the kiss." Britney placed her hand over her mouth. I could tell she forgot the cameras were on. She put her face in the pillow and said, "Oh no, now everybody is going to know."

I tried to console her. I looked into the camera, "We can cut that out, can't we?"

The cameraman shrugged his shoulders. Lily didn't say a word either. *Oops . . . sorry Britney.* My mom brought us pizza while we were watching the movie. "Girls, don't stay up too late."

"We won't," I assured her; although she knew I was lying because any night Britney and Sierra were staying would be a long night.

My cell phone rang. Normally, I would have let the call go to voice mail, but since the camera was rolling I answered it. "I really need to see you," William said.

"I told you to stop calling me. I don't want a boyfriend," I said and clicked the phone off. I looked into the camera. "That's some guy who keeps pestering me. I've told him I don't like him but he just won't stop calling."

"He's cuckoo for Cocoa Puffs, if you ask me," Britney said.

"I told you to block your number," Sierra said.

"If he calls back, I'm ignoring him."

My phone vibrated, alerting me I had a text message. I hit delete. I looked at the camera again and sounding annoyed, I said, "That was him."

After the cameramen and producers from the show left, we met up in my bedroom. "That was fun," Sierra said.

I agreed. It was good sharing the spotlight with my friends.

27

The Session

The next few days flew by as my parents went through televised counseling and Brenda and I were followed by a cameraman during our day-to-day activities. Dr. Marie Nelson wanted Brenda and me to sit in on a session and it would be televised. I was nervous because neither my parents nor Lily would let me know how my parents' counseling sessions were going.

Should I lie or tell the truth when asked certain questions? Would the counselor know if I was lying? Would she call me out for it? Did I really want to expose myself like this? Now I saw how my mom originally felt.

I took a few deep breaths and followed Brenda into the living room. My parents were sitting next to each other on the couch. They were not holding hands but they were sitting close. I sat next to my father and Brenda sat next to my mom. From the outside looking in, we looked like one big happy family.

Dr. Nelson stated, "I want to thank you two for supporting your parents the way that you have. I can tell family is very important to you both."

Brenda and I both shook our heads in agreement.

"Jasmine, since you're the youngest, first I want you to tell me how your parents bickering affects you."

"It doesn't."

"Jasmine. In order for me to help you . . . help your parents, I need you to be honest with me . . . with them." She looked in their direction. "Now look at them and tell them."

After almost thirty minutes of going back and forth, and a few shed tears, I finally admitted, "When you argue, it makes me feel like it's my fault."

My dad placed his arm around me and said, "Our arguments have nothing to do with you. Your mom and I have other issues. Grown-up issues that cause us to disagree."

My mom said, "Yes. That we can agree on. Jas, honey, the issues we've been dealing with aren't about you at all."

Dr. Nelson said, "You do understand that because

your parents are not getting along . . . that's their issue, not yours, right?"

I looked down. I didn't want to have another emotional breakdown in front of the cameras. "It sure doesn't feel that way," I said.

Dr. Nelson asked Brenda, "Do you feel like Jasmine?"

Brenda, trying to sound confident, said, "No. I'm old enough to know that sometimes it's best if parents go their separate ways."

"So you want your parents to break up?" It didn't sound like Dr. Nelson believed her.

Brenda said, "No, but it doesn't matter to me whether they stay together or not. I just want them both to be happy."

"I want them to be happy too . . . but together," I said.

My mom interjected and said, "Even if we're not together, we won't stop loving you."

Surprisingly, my dad and mom both agreed on something. He said, "You'll always be the apple of my eye. Nothing will destroy that love."

I could feel myself getting upset and before I realized it, I burst out and said, "Y'all act like your marriage is over. What was all of this for? Dad, you told me to never quit. Well, you're acting like a quitter."

I was so upset that I stormed out the room. My

mom followed me and unbeknown to me at the time, one of the cameramen was right behind her. "Jas, come back here. Our session is not over."

"For me it is. If you two aren't going to try, what's the point? I might as well go pack up my stuff now while y'all decide who I will live with."

I left her at the bottom of the stairway, upset. At this point I didn't care. All I knew was that all of my hard work seemed to be going down the drain. This was supposed to keep my family together. *Now what?* I threw myself across my bed.

A few minutes later, someone knocked on my door. "Who is it?" I yelled.

"Dr. Nelson. Can I come in?"

I got up and unlocked the door. "Sure," I responded, barely above a whisper.

Standing behind Dr. Nelson was a cameraman. She turned and said to him, "Give us a minute." She walked in my room. "Do you mind if we talk for a moment?"

"What about them?" I said, looking in the direction of the cameraman.

"This part won't be televised. Joe, you can take a break. We'll resume later," she told him. She closed the door so we could have some privacy.

"Have a seat," she said.

She was in my room but she acted like this was her office. I obeyed her, though.

I sat on the edge of my bed and she sat in my computer chair but turned the chair around to face my direction. "I realize this may be a difficult time for you. If you need to vent, let it out."

She was practically a stranger. What more did I have to say to her? My parents were jerks and I didn't care what they did? "My parents are selfish. That's all I have to say."

There was something about the gentleness in her eyes that had a calming effect on me as she talked. "Jasmine, your parents are two individuals who may or may not stay together. You must know that their relationship has nothing to do with their relationship with you."

"So are you saying that the counseling isn't working? That I need to prepare myself for the big split?"

"Only those two can answer whether they will remain together. What I want from you is for you to know in here—" she pointed at her head and then her heart—"that your parents love you and will love you regardless of what happens between the two of them."

"So are you ready to go back downstairs to our group session or should we try it another time?" she asked.

I had no idea I would get this emotional about things, but I knew I had to continue if it would change my parents' minds about divorcing. "I'm ready." I stood up.

"You're doing well. You're letting them know how you feel, so don't stop now, okay." She wrapped her arm around my shoulder and led me out of my room.

I tried to ignore the cameras as the eyes of my family stared up at us when we reentered the living room. This time I took a seat next to Brenda. It didn't go unnoticed by my dad because I could see the disappointment in his eyes. I looked away as Dr. Nelson resumed our group session.

Dr. Nelson said, "I want to encourage you all to keep open dialogue. Jasmine was honest about her feelings and you two need to recognize and deal with her feelings."

My dad said, "We've tried to explain to her."

Dr. Nelson interrupted him. "She might act like an adult at times, but Jasmine is still a child. You've explained it to her. If that didn't work, what you must do is try another way. I don't care how often. I don't mean to sound harsh, but this is your mess and you must clean it up."

I could see the tension in my dad's forehead. I could tell it was taking everything he had not to respond.

My mom smiled as if she got validation that all of their problems were caused by my dad.

Brenda said, "Jasmine has to learn that everything isn't always about her."

My mom reprimanded Brenda. "Bren, that's enough."

Brenda snapped, "I'm just telling the truth. If you both would stop spoiling her, then she would realize your situation wasn't about her."

I said, in between clenched teeth, "Tell everybody how you really feel."

Brenda went on to say, "Jas, I love you, but you are spoiled rotten."

My dad came to my defense. "Like you aren't. The problem is I've spoiled all of you girls—your mom included."

My mom said, "Dion, you act like you were doing us a favor. You're the head of the household. You're supposed to take care of your family."

"Kim, I know my responsibilities. I have always taken care of my family and will continue to do so." He looked at the doctor and said, "See, this is one of our biggest problems right here. Kim is always taking what I say out of context and the next thing you know we're arguing about something that's really not important."

"No, Doctor, it's Dion. He thinks because he's the major breadwinner, he can talk to me any kind of way. But that's not happening." By now my mom was standing up. She's five feet five with heels on, so you can imagine how crazy she looked standing in front of my still bulky-looking dad.

"Kim, sit down. We can talk about this calmly," Dr. Nelson said.

My mom stepped over my dad's feet and went to sit on the love seat. Being cocky, he said, "See, this is typical Kim. She walks around with a chip on her shoulder and acts like everybody is supposed to bow down to her every whim. She's a drama queen, so don't expect her to act rationally."

"The truth is coming out now, isn't it? See, this is the real Dion. The one his fans don't get to see. Y'all see how he talks to me," my mom said, looking into the camera. "You need to show some respect and maybe we could get along better."

Dr. Nelson had lost her control over them. I leaned back in my chair and watched him and my mom go back and forth. The camera was tuned right on them. I'm pretty sure they wouldn't be editing this part out. I just hoped that by the end of taping, I could walk away with a little dignity because they were embarrassing me. To think I thought filming a reality show was a good idea.

28

A Little Bit of This and That

The previous day's group session didn't go well, but I was hoping that their one-on-one session would go better. If not, I would have to give up all hope of them staying together. I expressed my concerns to Britney and Sierra over lunch. "Y'all should have seen it. I was too embarrassed."

Sierra said, "Just wait until they air it. You're really going to be embarrassed then."

"Thank you for reminding me," I said, now regretting that I ever sent in their application.

Britney pulled out her BlackBerry and showed me the screen. "They are already showing previews online. Girl, you look good in the promos."

"Already," I said. I didn't realize they would be advertising the show this soon. They weren't through filming. They had only been doing it a few weeks.

Britney said, "According to this, the first show airs next week."

I scrolled down the screen. *Oh my goodness.* My life is about to change forever. Why did I insist we do the show?

"Are you ready for your fan mail?" Britney asked, sounding excited.

"I hope some cute guys e-mail you . . . what am I talking about—us. We're going to be on an episode too," Sierra said, joining in on the excitement.

"If they don't edit us out," Britney said.

"Is it true you're going to be on TV," DJ walked over to our table and interrupted us.

"Stay out of my business and I'll stay out of yours," I responded.

"I wonder what McNeil would say once he realizes his daughter is the school's slut," he said as he walked away.

I jumped out of my seat to hit him. It took Britney and Sierra both to hold me down and that's saying much, since I was shorter than the both of them. "I'm going to get him."

"Calm down. You deal with your parents. We'll deal with DJ," Britney said.

"But . . . what if he goes through with his threat? I

don't want my daddy thinking I'm a slut," I said. I slid back in my seat and placed my hand on my aching stomach.

Sierra said, "We'll keep an eye out on him so don't worry about it."

"I think I'm getting an ulcer," I said, as I looked up the symptoms of having an ulcer on my cell phone. "Okay, I don't have an ulcer. According to this, it might be gas."

Britney wiggled her nose and said, "Time for me to go. I don't have any air freshener with me." We all laughed.

As we walked by DJ's table, he was all smiles. I mouthed the words, *Don't mess with me or you'll be sorry.* His smile faded.

Once we were outside of the cafeteria, Britney said, "Forget DJ. We have a premiere party to plan for."

Sierra added, "I can't wait. I'm telling everybody I know about the show."

"Me too." Britney's tone changed to excitement. "My mom's excited about it. She has an appearance on the show since she's your mom's best friend."

"My mom is going to be so jealous because I don't think she was asked."

"Maybe I shouldn't have said anything," Britney regretfully said.

"She'll get over it. At least I'm on there," Sierra stated.

We talked about our plans for our premiere party until it was time for us to go to our individual classes.

Brenda had a test, so after school, Britney's driver dropped me off at home. The driveway was empty so that meant there would be no one filming. For once, I was glad not to be in the spotlight.

My phone rang before I could get to my room. I fumbled trying to get to it without dropping my stuff. "Is this Jasmine?" a sexy baritone voice said from the other end.

"Who is this?" I asked. I was in my room. I threw my book bag on the bed and removed my shoes.

"Benjamin."

I laid my back down on the bed and looked at the ceiling as we talked. "It sure took you awhile to call." I turned over and looked at the calendar. I counted the weeks since the Valentine's dance. It was now March.

"I was scared to call."

"You must have gotten over your fear, so why are you calling now?"

"I really wanted to talk to you. I've been going to church with Travis, but haven't seen you."

"That's because I haven't been there."

"Are you all right?"

I sat up. "I'm fine. My folks are going through some things and haven't been bringing me."

"If you need a ride, I can have my brother come by and pick you up," he said.

"That's sweet of you, but I'll be there Sunday. If you come, I'll see you then."

We chatted for a few more minutes. I wasn't feeling Benjamin like I was the first night I met him. Maybe if he would have called me sooner, but now I had lost interest. He still seemed like a nice guy, but I didn't think he was the one.

I pulled out my homework and knocked it out before dinner. I wasn't aware that I was still home alone until I left to go downstairs and the whole house was dark. I'm not a scared person but it felt eerie, walking around a dark house. I flipped on every light I passed and went to the kitchen to see if I could find some leftovers.

I didn't see anything appetizing in the refrigerator, but grabbed a can of soda. I sensed someone was in the room and jumped, almost hitting my head on the refrigerator shelf. "Mom, you scared me. I didn't hear you walk in," I said.

She stood on the other side of the refrigerator door. "I got dinner, so you can put whatever junk you got back in there."

I closed the door. "I only have a soda."

"Grab some plates and meet me in the dining room."

"Are you by yourself?"

"It'll be just the two of us," she responded from a distance.

I grabbed some plates and silverwear. I placed the soda under my arm.

"Oh, you're not going to get your mama a drink?"

"Sorry, Mom." I rushed back to the kitchen and returned with her drink and a glass of ice.

"Destiny went into false labor so I'm just coming from the hospital," she said as she fixed our plates.

"What? Britney didn't tell me." I was mad at Britney now. She was my best friend and she didn't call to tell me her mom was in the hospital.

"She didn't know. We were filming and she started having these pains, so we rushed her to the hospital. The doctor let her go home, so I just dropped her off."

"I have to call Britney. I'm sure she was freaking out."

"Young lady, you're going to eat your dinner first."

"Yes, ma'am." I was too excited to eat. I needed to find out from Britney how things were going. Mothers never tell you everything.

"There are my two favorite girls," my dad said as

he entered the room. He kissed me on the cheek and tried to kiss my mom, but she pushed him away.

He grabbed a piece of chicken out of the box. My mom said, "I hope you washed your hands."

"I'm a grown man, if I want to eat my food without washing my hands, that's my prerogative."

"That's nasty. Dion, you need help."

"Woman, don't talk to me like that."

I was just glad the cameras weren't around to record another round of the Dion and Kim show.

I finished eating and left them in the dining room, arguing. Those two were wearing me out.

I dialed Britney's number by the time I got to my room. "Are you okay? Is your mom okay?" I asked questions, not bothering to wait for her to respond.

"My dad's the one that's having a fit. He keeps getting on both of our nerves," she responded.

I listened to her tell her version of her mom's hospital stay.

"You'll be a big sister soon," I teased.

"I'm just glad this was a false alarm."

Britney was used to being an only child and from our conversations she wasn't too happy about sharing the spotlight. I can't say I blame her. Being the baby of our family, I thrived on the attention.

29

Ratings

The *Situation Number Nine* online message boards were hopping. We had our own Web site . . . well, my parents did, but Brenda and I were in the family portrait displayed on the Web site. They even showed a few behind-the-scenes clips with me and my girls talking about boys and lip gloss. I was surprised at how many people were interested in an ex–football player's life. If he was still playing football, we would have quadrupled the interest, I'm sure.

We had the premiere party over at Britney's since her mom wasn't supposed to be traveling anywhere. All of our parents and some of their friends were in the place. Overall, it had to be fifty people crowded into the mini–movie studio room at the Franklins.

Britney, Sierra, and a few of my cousins as well as Brenda and her friends sat in the back.

"Pass me the butter," Brenda said as she chewed on her popcorn.

"I thought you were cutting down on butter products," Britney asked.

"That was last semester," Brenda said and went back to talking to her friends.

"Shhh. The show's about to start," my mom said.

Britney's dad turned down the lights and we looked like we were really at a movie theater, as the show started playing on the huge television screen. I had to admit, we all looked good on screen. Nicholas told the audience the rules for the show. "The goal of *Situation Number Nine* is to save a family from being destroyed. This season we're helping America's favorite Cowboy, Dion McNeil."

I moved to the edge of my seat and watched. I tuned out everybody around me as I concentrated on the show.

"That Nicholas is so cute," Sierra said.

"He's not as nice as I thought he would be," I commented.

"Ladies, hold it down," Destiny Franklin said.

Either everybody here was nosy or they really were interested in supporting my folks. They all clapped when the show ended. I didn't see anything on the screen to clap about. My stupid idea had my family fully exposed and now I would have to deal with it.

"Girl, I didn't know your mama was like that," one of my cousins said.

"Yeah, no wonder you act like you think you're better than us," another cousin said.

"Whatever." I rolled my eyes. It took a lot for me not to slap both of them. I was doing my best to keep the peace. They were jealous and as much as they liked to complain, they were the first ones to arrive whenever my mom or dad invited them to a function.

"See, just like your mama with that uppity attitude."

Brenda overhead them and said, "April, you need to chill with the comments."

April rolled her eyes at Brenda once Brenda had turned around. I looked at her. She wasn't my favorite cousin, but she was my mom's sister's child so I dealt with her whenever we had a family function. So I wouldn't hit her or her sister, I left the room. Britney and Sierra followed me.

"Your cousin April is a trip," Sierra said.

We were standing outside on the patio. "I know. I can't stand her sometimes," I said.

My mom walked out. "So what did you girls think about the first show?"

Britney and Sierra looked at each other. *I guess I'm the spokesman.* I said, "I wished you and dad didn't argue so much, but other than that, you looked great."

She wrapped her arm around my shoulder. "This thing was your idea. We only did it to please you."

"Yeah, I know. I should have stayed out of it."

She leaned down closer to my face. "What did you say? Did I hear you correctly?"

I didn't deny, so I repeated myself.

"Girls, you heard her, didn't you? My baby admitted she was wrong."

"Mom," I said. I liked being the center of attention but not if it wasn't in a favorable light.

"Just kidding, baby. The counseling did help us."

My eyes lit up. "So you're staying together?"

"I'm not sure . . . but at least this has helped."

I hugged my mom. There was hope for my family after all. We followed her back in the house and enjoyed the festivities. I avoided April and her sister for the rest of the night. I didn't need their negativity to spoil my family's celebration.

I watched my parents and although they weren't arguing, they kept their distance from one another. It didn't take a reality show for me to see what was staring me right in the face. The chances or the reality of them staying together was slim to none. I slid down in my chair as if I accepted defeat. I wasn't a quitter and until they signed some divorce papers, there was still hope. At least that's what I told myself.

"Pip-squeak, I'm glad you talked them into doing the show," Brenda said as she hit me on the arm.

I sat up. "They seem happy about it, but I don't know."

"Stop overanalyzing stuff and just enjoy the moment," she said before walking away.

My phone vibrated. I answered. Benjamin was on the other end. "I didn't know your dad was *the* Dion McNeil."

I listened to him go on and on about my dad's football statistics. "Ben—" I didn't bother to ask him if it was okay for me to shorten his name. "I'm with some friends right now so I got to go." I hung up on him without waiting for him to respond.

My phone rang again. This time it was Cecil. "I can't believe I've been tutoring McNeil's daughter. Man, this is so cool."

I laughed. Cecil's excitement didn't irritate me like Benjamin's did. "I'm still the same ol' Jasmine."

"I know, but you didn't tell me. You could have told me."

"Would that have changed anything?" I asked.

"No, but it would have been nice to know."

"Well, now you know, but Cecil, I'll talk to you at school tomorrow. It's getting kind of loud and I can barely hear you."

My phone rang again. I had definitely become Ms. Popular. I didn't recognize the number. "You looked good in that green."

"Who is this?"

"You forgot about me already. I know I shouldn't have stopped calling," William said.

"William, I'm glad you thought I was cute, but I told you I didn't want to talk to you again. Nothing's changed."

"You'll want me."

"What is that supposed to mean?" I asked. He was really spoiling my mood.

"You'll find out," he said, and laughed. His laugh made my skin crawl. I didn't have to hang up on him, because he ended the call.

"Ugh. Why are you looking like that?" Britney said as she sat down across from me.

"That was William. He's so weird."

"Girl, forget him. How do you like being a celebrity?"

I held out my phone. "I'll tell you after I get my phone call from Soulja Boy."

She laughed. "I guess I'll never know because you'll be waiting a long time on that phone call."

My dad got everybody's attention and shouted, "One of the producers just called me. We had the highest rating in our time slot."

Cheers were heard around the room. I looked for my mom but didn't see her at first. She was standing near the door with a fake smile plastered across her face. She held up her glass as if she was cheering too. My Aunt Carla and her daughters made a beeline straight to where she stood. I could tell my mom was just going through the motions, because at this moment, so was I.

30

Push Back

I got up early the next day and checked the entertainment and gossip blogs and we were the talk of the Internet. It felt good being in the spotlight. I was glad to see the fashion police liked the outfits I had on. Now I had official validation on my fashion choices. I bookmarked the links and got ready for school.

I was in a good mood until I got to school and ran into DJ. "I saw you last night," he said as I kept on walking up the walkway toward the doors.

I ignored him, but it didn't do any good because he kept talking. "I'm going online when I get home and let everybody know about McNeil's daughter."

I stopped walking and took my book bag off my arm and hauled off and hit him. Britney or Sierra were not around to stop me. I must have caught him by surprise because it was a few seconds before he tried to retaliate. I kicked him and he tried his best to push me off. One of the teachers came and pulled us apart. "What's going on here?" he asked.

"She started attacking me with her backpack," DJ screamed.

DJ was at least ten inches taller than me so the teacher didn't believe him.

"He was messing with me so I was just protecting myself," I responded.

No one would confirm or deny what either one of us said. "You two can go to the office . . . now."

DJ was mad. I was mad. I rolled my eyes at him as we were lead to the principal's office. The principal was out, so we had to wait on Mr. Reese.

"Ms. McNeil, don't think you'll be getting any special treatment because of your daddy," he said.

I willed myself not to roll my eyes. I willed myself to keep my mouth shut because the things going through my head about him would definitely get me in trouble. He was jealous because he probably couldn't throw a football; probably wasn't married because who would marry someone who grated their nerves.

DJ and I listened to him give us a lecture about

proper school behavior. "I'm really supposed to suspend both of you, but since I'm in a nice mood this morning, I will just give you detention."

"Detention," DJ burst out. "I have practice after school. I don't have time for detention."

I remained quiet. Mr. Reese said, "You're lucky I'm not kicking you off the team."

Oh, I get it. He's a jock lover, so he's letting us off easy because of DJ. It figures.

He looked at me. "This is the second time this year I've seen you. Let it be your last or the next time I will have to suspend you."

"Yes sir," I said as I saluted him.

"All of that's not necessary. Get your hall pass from the receptionist and get to class." He looked at DJ and then back again at me. "Both of you. Now get out and stop all of that fighting."

DJ and I both made it to the entryway of the door at the same time. Surprisingly, he moved and allowed me to go through first. I didn't want him behind me, so I said, "No, you go."

We left the office and went in opposite directions. Britney and Sierra tried to make eye contact with me when I made it to Mrs. Johnson's class, but I avoided looking at them. I handed the teacher my pass and slipped into my chair.

"Because of your ex-man, I got detention," I told Sierra after class. I told them about the incident in front of the school.

Sierra found it funny. "Girl, I wish I would have been there to see it."

"I'm surprised he didn't just knock you down," Britney said.

"He knows better."

"That's too bad you got detention for it," Sierra said.

By now we were at the end of the hall where we were about to go our separate ways. "I'll be fine. It'll give me a chance to do my homework without distractions."

All through the day, different people who had never spoken to me were stopping me and asking me questions. I guess word had gotten out about the show. During lunch, I left my new fans to go sit with the girls I knew had my back. They were there before and they would be there when things calmed down.

Cecil stopped by our table. "Can I sit with y'all?" he asked.

I looked at Britney and Sierra as they waited on my response. "Sure. I'm in a good mood today."

Cecil had to backtrack. He probably thought I was going to tell him no, because he was about to walk away. He took a few steps backward and sat his tray down at our table. I moved my stuff over to give him some room.

"I have detention for getting into it with Dylan Johnson earlier, so don't look for me to call you this evening," I said.

"I saw the fight. I know not to mess with you," he teased.

"He had it coming. He's always messing with somebody."

"Don't feel bad, he messes with me too."

Sierra and Britney remained quiet as Cecil and I talked. "The only reason why he talks to you like that, Cecil, is because you let him."

"I don't like confrontation."

"But if you don't stand up for yourself, he'll keep doing it," I said.

He stared at his food. "You're probably right."

I tapped him on the arm. "You can do it. Besides, I got your back." I smiled and winked at him.

Before we all left to go our separate ways to class, I said to Cecil, "What's the word for today?"

He responded, "Push back."

31

More Pushing

In between classes, I called my mom and told her about the fight with DJ. "You can't go around hitting on boys, Jasmine."

"He was asking for it."

"I'm taking away your laptop for a week."

Whenever my mom wanted to punish me, she would take my laptop. Now I really was pissed. "I need my computer to do some of my homework."

"You can do your homework on my computer."

"But, Mom—"

"But Mom nothing. Next time think twice before you act. You're a young lady; you can't be fighting in public."

I wanted to say, *Like you and Dad*, but I was already being punished for a week so I didn't want to push it.

"Mom, if I don't get off the phone I'm going to be late for class," I said as I interrupted her mini-lecture.

In between classes, I was answering questions about the show. I barely beat the tardy bell for detention. DJ looked up and smiled at me. I rolled my eyes and gave him the finger, not caring who saw me. I found a seat on the opposite side of the room from him.

Some people were asking me if I was the same chick that was on that show that came on the night before. DJ wouldn't give me a chance to respond. "Yes. You know she and I used to hang out."

"I need you all to get in your seats and do your work. If you don't have any homework, pretend like you do. This is not a time to socialize," Ms. Houston said as she walked down each row.

An hour later, I was standing outside waiting on Brenda to pick me up. I called her but she wouldn't answer her phone. DJ walked by me. I hoped he didn't say anything, but my luck ran out. "You know, if you didn't have such a funky attitude you would be all right."

I threw my hand in the air and said, "Whatever."

"I'm just saying. Maybe you and I can start over." I wanted to slap the smug look off his face.

"Mr. Johnson, don't you think you need to be getting home," Ms. Houston walked up behind us and said.

"Thanks," I said, once he started walking away.

"I don't know what to say about these young men these days."

"He's the reason why I got detention so I'm really not trying to deal with him," I said.

"Between you and me, DJ is a bully and I don't like the way he treats girls so you did the right thing by standing up for yourself."

Brenda zoomed in front of the school. "There's my sister. Thanks, Ms. Houston."

"What took you so long?" I asked. I threw my backpack in the backseat and hopped up front.

"You getting detention threw off my schedule so don't be complaining," she responded.

"It's not like it was planned."

"What's that noise?" she asked.

It was my phone beeping. It was in my backpack. I undid my seat belt so I could reach it. It was a missed call from Britney. I dialed her back. She sounded out of breath. "My mom's on the way to the hospital. I think she's about to have the babies," she said.

I touched Brenda's arm, scaring her. "We got to get to the hospital. Britney's mom is about to have the babies."

"I'm taking you home."

"No, you have to take me to the hospital."

"I don't even know what hospital they'll be at."

"Mama knows. Let me call her." I called our mom. After hanging up, I told Brenda, "She says you can drop me off at Presbyterian if you don't want to stay."

"I'll do just that, because I don't like hospitals. Do you want something to eat before I get on the toll-way?"

"No. I'll eat something later." I was too excited.

I tried calling Britney back but she didn't answer her phone. I called Sierra, "Did you hear? I'm on my way to the hospital now," I said.

"I don't have a way but be sure to call me when she has the babies and take some pics." Sierra sounded just as excited as I was.

Riding with Brenda was like riding in the back of a speeding ambulance. We were at the hospital in no time. "Call me when she has the babies," Brenda said before I exited the car.

I asked the guard for directions. I knew I found it when I saw Mr. Franklin pacing the floor. My mom had her arm around Britney's shoulder. "Did she have them yet?" I asked.

"Hey, dear. No, she's in the delivery room right now."

Before she could say anything else, a doctor came out. "Mr. Franklin, can I talk to you for a minute?"

I watched Britney's dad rush over to the doctor. I couldn't hear the conversation, but the look that swept across Mr. Franklin's face didn't look good. Britney jumped up and rushed over to where he stood. "Dad, what's wrong with Mom?"

Barely above a whisper, he responded, "They're having problems. Apparently one of the babies is blocking them both from entering the world."

"Oh no," Britney said.

"Kim, can you make sure Britney will be okay? I'm going to the delivery room."

"Go ahead. Don't worry about her. I'm here."

I placed my arm around Britney as she started crying. "It's all my fault. I didn't want a sister or brother."

My mom got up to console her too. "Dear, it's not your fault."

"Yes, it is. I told God I wanted to be an only child."

I moved out the way so my mom could talk to her because I didn't know what to say. My mom said, "These types of things are common any time there are multiple births."

Britney acted like she didn't believe her and wouldn't stop crying. My mom motioned for me to come near. I wrapped my arm around her. "Bri, the babies will be fine. You'll see. This time next year, we'll be taking them shopping with us." That was the only thing I could think to say.

"This happened because I'm selfish. Ms. Pearl told me I needed to stop being selfish and now look what happened."

My mom had us hold hands as she prayed out loud. We consoled Britney as much as we could. Sierra called a few times to see how things were going. I couldn't really say what I wanted to say, so I hung up with her and sent her a text message. While I was typing my last text response, Mr. Franklin showed back up in the waiting room.

Britney, who had been lying down, shot up and ran to him. "Are they here? Tell me they're all right."

His facial expression lacked any emotion at this point. My heart dropped as I waited for Mr. Franklin to respond to Britney.

"Come here, baby," he said as Britney ran into his arms and they held each other.

"Mama," I whispered.

She rubbed my back. "It's going to be okay, baby. It has to be."

I prayed silent prayers as we waited what seemed like an eternity for the doctors to come out and give us a status report.

Mr. Franklin rose out of his seat as soon as he saw the doctor.

"It was rough going, but mother and babies are both doing okay. One of them will have to be on oxygen."

"Can I see them?" Mr. Franklin asked.

"Not right now. They're getting all cleaned up. Once we get them situated in the prenatal unit, you can visit them both."

"Can I at least see Destiny?"

"Yes, she's a little groggy but she's been asking for you."

"Come on, Britney."

Britney followed him through the swinging doors.

I think I let out the loudest sigh of relief. If anything had happened to those babies, I don't know what I would have done with Britney. She was normally the calm one, but this evening she had broken down and we had to be the ones to console her. Who would have thought having babies would cause this much drama?

32

Two For One

"The babies are going to need a lot of TLC," my mom said over breakfast the next morning to Britney. Britney had spent the night over at our house. She would be going to the hospital with my mom, after they dropped me off at school.

"Yes, ma'am. I plan on doing my part. I'm glad they're here."

"Your mom will be happy to hear that," she said, smiling in between bites.

I tried to get out of going to school, but since I had detention my mom wasn't hearing it. Sierra was already sitting at her desk when I made it to homeroom. Since we had a few minutes before the bell would ring, I sat next to her and told her about last night's events.

"Talk about nervous. I thought for sure something bad was going to happen," I said.

"I did too but I prayed and prayed after you sent me that text message."

"God heard our prayers," I said, right before Mrs. Johnson came into class. I went to take my seat because I wasn't trying to get into any more trouble.

I raised my hand to get her attention. "Yes, Jasmine."

"Britney won't be here today because her mom had her babies."

"Are they doing okay?"

"One of the babies is on a ventilator, but the other one is doing okay."

"Dang, how many babies did she have?" a girl in the back of the class asked.

"None of your business," Mrs. Johnson answered for me. She looked at me. "Tell her to have her dad call me, okay."

"Yes, ma'am."

I heard the boy behind me whisper, "Teacher's pet."

I turned around and stuck my tongue out at him. Mrs. Johnson looked at me over the rim of her glasses. I sunk down in my chair and started reading over my lesson.

My grades in algebra had improved drastically. My

teacher seemed amazed as she handed me another A paper. I was thrilled. All of the time invested in being tutored had paid off. I placed the paper in front of Cecil when I met up with him during study period.

"You're not going to need me any more," he said, sounding disappointed.

"We can still hang out every now and then," I responded. I opened up my book to the problem I needed his immediate help on. "We can start by you helping me with that word problem on page one-twenty-eight."

"It's not complicated at all. All you need to do is make sure you remember the formula from last week."

He spent the next ten minutes walking me through the problem. I felt confident that I had the hang of it, so I completed the rest of it by the end of study period. We made a copy of it for him, so he could check it later and call me or e-mail me if I did some of them wrong. Our little system had worked for us, so why change now?

"Cheerleader tryouts are coming up," Sierra told me over lunch.

"When, because I need to practice some of my moves."

"In a few weeks."

"I've been so caught up in my parents' life that I forgot all about tryouts."

"You got time."

"I haven't worked out like I should."

"My dance teacher is keeping me limber," she responded.

"I need to stop eating this cafeteria food too because I've gained a few pounds."

"I can't tell," she responded.

"You wouldn't be able to with these uniforms, but trust me, I have."

Sierra looked at her phone. "That's Britney."

"Tell her I said hi."

While Britney talked to Sierra, my eyes wandered to where Cecil was sitting with his friends. Our eyes locked. It's like he had me in a trance. I couldn't look away. When I saw him, I saw a cute boy who was smarter than anybody I knew. His eyes sparkled. When he smiled, I saw the crevice of his dimples. I winked at him and then looked away.

"Bri says one of the twins might be able to go home tomorrow. Precious won't be able to go home until they make sure she breathes on her own."

I didn't respond to Sierra. She put her hand up and down in front of my face. "Earth to Jas. Are you listening?"

"Yes. What was that? The twins might be home to-morrow."

She repeated herself. "What—or should I say *who*—has your attention?" She looked in the same direction I was looking and then turned back around. "Who? I don't see anyone?"

"What do you think about Cecil?" I asked.

"He's all right, I guess," she responded.

"Isn't he cute in a nerdy sort of way?"

"Actually, I don't look at him as being a nerd. He's always been cute to me."

"Really." I perked up. "Then why didn't you ever say anything?"

"I said he was cute, not that I wanted to holler at him."

"So would you date him?"

"No, because I know you like him. And we're not going down that road again."

"I don't like him. He's just my tutor. A friend."

Sierra looked at me like she doubted what I was telling her. I defended myself. "I'm for real. He's just a friend."

"The way you've been looking at him lately has me wondering how close a friend he is," she commented.

"Don't even go there."

Sierra sighed. "Oh, I wasn't even thinking about

that. At first you didn't even want him to talk to you . . . but now . . . you even let him have lunch with us."

"I thought I liked more of the athletic type, but you know what, I can dig a boy who got brains. Cecil is all right with me."

"So when are you going to let him know that?"

"I'm not."

"But you just said—"

I interrupted her. "Just because I like a boy, it doesn't mean I'm going to let him know I like him."

"Is that something Brenda taught you?" Sierra asked in a sarcastic tone.

"No. That's something I read in one of Brenda's books."

"I need a copy of it." I could hear the excitement in her voice.

"I'll bring it tomorrow. It's a lot of good stuff in it. You have to give it back to me next week, though, before she realizes it's missing."

"Sure. I can't wait to read it," Sierra said as her eyes lit up.

"Here comes Britney's ex," I said as Marcus walked up to our table.

"I just stopped by to tell you that you need to check the message board at *Situation Number Nine*'s site. It seems you have an obsessed fan on there."

"I hope it's not your cousin because if it is, I swear

I'll have my parents sue his parents." It wasn't just a threat. I was serious.

"I don't think it was him, but he was the one who told me about it. I thought I should warn you, with you being Britney's friend and all."

"Okay thanks, I think." The thought of DJ or any other dude saying bad stuff about me on the message board made me upset.

I tried to log on to the Internet from my Black-Berry but the server was down.

"Girl, I need to get to the library before lunch ends," I said anxiously to Sierra.

"I'll get your tray. I'll meet you in there," she said.

I rushed to the library and found an empty com-puter. I hoped there wasn't a block from the televi-sion stations Web site so I could view the message board. I set the search button to identify every time my name popped up.

"Bingo," I said out loud.

Sierra had pulled up a chair by now. She said, "You better hurry, the bell is about to ring."

We read some of the comments on the thread.

ASecretAdmirer: Jasmine I love you. You make
                 my heart beat faster every
                 time I see you in the hallway.
                 (6:59 PM)

ASecretAdmirer: Jasmine why aren't you
                  responding to any of my
                  messages? Don't you know
                  we're meant to be together?
                  (7:30 PM)

ASecretAdmirer: DON'T IGNORE ME. What
                  would your daddy say if he
                  knew his little girl did some
                  adult things. He wouldn't be
                  too happy about that now
                  would he? (8:00 PM)

"That has to be DJ, because that sounds like something he said to me earlier." I was livid. What if my parents read this? I could strangle him.

Sierra sounded just as convinced as I was that it was DJ. "And he has been spreading rumors about you, but nobody has been paying him any attention."

"So now that I'm on the show, he wants to go national with his mess. Oh, wait until I see him."

We strolled through some of the other messages. I copied them and sent them to myself in e-mail. The bell rang, alerting us it was time to go to our class. "I'll call you later. I want to go see the babies when Brenda picks me up."

"I'll ask my mom if I can tag along, so check your text messages when you get out of class."

While walking to class, I sent Brenda a text message about the messages on the board. DJ would be sorry he ever met me when my folks got through.

33

More Problems

After detention, Sierra and I went to see the twins. My mom actually took us because Brenda had a late exam. "Aren't they the cutest little things?" my mom said as we watched them through the window in the prenatal unit.

"How long will Precious have to be on that breathing machine?" I asked.

"Until the doctor's sure she can breathe on her own," Britney responded.

We left my mom and went to the hospital cafeteria. We caught Britney up on what had happened at school. Sierra couldn't wait to tell her about my secret crush on Cecil. "I knew it before you did," she told Sierra.

"Whatever," I said. "I can handle Cecil, but what I'm having a problem with is DJ. He's gone too far now."

Sierra said, "While you were in detention, I did some research on the Internet. If we can prove that it was DJ, he could get some jail time."

"What? Then he'll be out of our hair forever." I felt like doing cartwheels.

"But what if it isn't him? Then you'll mess up his chances of going to college," Britney cautioned, once again being the voice of reason.

"You know what. I don't care at this point. He should have never started harassing me and then I wouldn't have thought it was him."

While my mom was dropping off Sierra, I thought about our earlier conversation in the hospital cafeteria. The secret admirer had to be DJ or else there was some other jerk out there. Lily's car was parked in front of the house when we got there. Before we exited the car, I said, "Mom, there's something I need to tell you."

"I know. I was just waiting to see how long it would take you."

"But you didn't say anything about it."

"The hospital was not the place for it. I am the one

who contacted Lily. She stopped by tonight to ask you a few questions. We need to find out who this person is."

"I'm so embarrassed," I said as I gathered my stuff and got out of the car.

"You don't have anything to be embarrassed about. We have no control over other people. Just ourselves."

When we got inside the house, my dad, Brenda, Lily, and a man who I hadn't seen before was sitting in the living room.

My dad got up and walked toward me. "Jasmine, this is Agent Forest. I called him once your mom told me about the messages."

Man, this was serious. He must be with the FBI or something. I was now beginning to think everybody was overreacting—including myself.

I took a seat next to my dad as the agent and Lily asked me questions. "Have you been receiving any annoying calls?"

"Yes, but it was from some boy I met back in January. He's not a problem."

The agent wrote something on a notepad. "What's his name?"

"William."

"Last name," he asked.

"I'm not sure."

My dad said, "What do you mean, you're not sure?"

"It was some boy I met on the Internet, okay. He goes by the screen name TallandFly."

My mom threw her hands up in the air and said, "Lord, my child almost got abducted by some pervert on the Internet."

If the situation wasn't so serious, my mom's antics would have been funny. "Mom, calm down. He wasn't a pervert. He was just some boy who went to Roosevelt High."

Brenda said, "I told you about chatting with strangers on the Internet."

I said, "I don't even think it was him. I think it's this guy from school."

Lily said, "Oh really. Tell us more."

I explained to them how DJ had been harassing me and my friends. Agent Forest's hands were writing fast. "What's DJ's real name?"

"Dylan Johnson and his phone number is 972-555-9234. I don't know his address."

"I have all the information I need, Mr. and Mrs. McNeil. We'll get right on this and I'll be calling you."

My dad walked him to the door. Lily said, "We've disabled the message boards temporarily. The police said we should put it back online just in case he's crazy enough to leave some more messages."

"What's going to happen to DJ if he is the one who sent me messages?" I asked.

My dad, in an angry tone, said, "His butt is going to jail. Jasmine, why didn't you tell us he was harassing you sooner? Some of this may have been avoided."

I looked at him and then at my mother. "You wouldn't have heard me. You two seem to have enough problems of your own than to worry about my problems."

My mom said, "Dion, she's right. We should have been paying our child more attention. Just to think that something could have happened to her. Come here, baby."

I walked to where my mom stood as she cradled me in her arms. I heard my dad say, "Lily, thanks for all your help and for jumping on this situation when Kim called you."

"We frown on this type of behavior, especially when it's directed toward a minor."

He said, "I can deal with folks saying stuff about me, but not about my kids. That's where I draw the line."

"Me too," she responded.

"I guess I'll see you in the morning," he said as he walked her out. He came back in the room and said, "I hope DJ's parents have a lot of money because after I see that he's put behind bars, I'm suing them."

34

Juice Please

"Please, don't hurt me. I won't tell anyone, I promise. Please," I yelled, kicking and screaming as the masked man tried to pin me down to the ground.

"Jasmine . . . Jasmine . . . wake up," my mom said, shaking me out of my sleep.

"Mama," I said, grabbing on to her as I woke up.

She brushed the hair out of my eyes. "You were having a bad dream. I'm right here."

"I'm sorry about the Internet thing," I said as she rocked me in her arms.

"Don't you know you can talk to me about anything?"

"But I thought you had enough to deal with. Besides, I didn't think it was that serious," I responded, still feeling embarrassed about the whole situation.

By now, we were sitting face-to-face. In a concerned tone, she said, "There are too many perverts on the Internet. You never know who's on the other end of that computer screen."

I told her about what happened the day I was supposed to meet William at the mall. "See, Britney and Sierra were with me. Nothing would have happened."

"You don't know that."

"I still think it's DJ. William hasn't called me in a few days."

"But you've told him to stop calling you, period, but yet he still keeps contacting you. His behavior reminds me of a stalker."

"Is Dad still here?" I asked.

"Yes, he's downstairs on the phone talking to Agent Forest."

"Can I stay home from school today?"

"Not a chance, young lady. I'll drive you myself. I think I've been neglecting you too much lately and that's why this is happening."

It was now my turn to console her. "Mom, it's not your fault. Like I said, I really think it's DJ. This is his way of getting me back for not talking to him."

She stood up and pulled the covers all the way

back. "Be careful and get up and get ready. You're already going to be late."

I rushed and got ready for school. My dad decided to come with us, so I sat in the backseat. He kept looking at me in the rearview mirror. I was curious to what he and Agent Forest had talked about, so I asked, "Did DJ get picked up last night?"

"No. And I don't want you talking to him today about it either," my dad snapped.

My mom said, "Don't take out your frustrations on Jasmine."

I couldn't understand why he was mad at me. It wasn't my fault that DJ and TallandFly were creeps.

"Something told me not to do that show . . . but no. I listened to you . . . and my agent . . . who, by the way, I'm firing. The cable show said they wanted another person to host their new sports show."

"I'm sorry, baby. I know how important that job was to you."

"Yeah. Apparently, I have too much drama going on in my household. They saw that from only one show."

"Who doesn't have drama?" My mom went from sounding concerned to getting an attitude.

"Well, regardless . . . this whole thing has just blown up in my face. Now I have to deal with some sicko trying to mess with my daughter. Somebody is going to pay for this."

I could feel the tension as we drove the rest of the way to school, listening to the *Steve Harvey Morning Show*. My father escorted me to the office. Any other time, I would have been proud to show off my dad, but I really didn't want additional attention after the night I had. "Dad, thanks for walking me in, but I'll be okay."

"I know you will. I've taught you how to take care of yourself," he said, leaning down and kissing me on the forehead.

Mr. Reese happened to walk out of the office as we were about to depart. He said, "Mr. McNeil, my receptionist told me you were out here. Can I talk to you for a minute?" He looked at me. I looked away.

"Go on to class, Jasmine. I'll see you later at home," my dad said.

I heard my dad tell Mr. Reese, "You're the man I need to see. I need to talk to you about Jasmine's detention."

Before lunch, one of my teachers handed me a written statement from the office stating I no longer had to report to detention. *Yes!* I don't know what my dad said to Mr. Reese, but my afternoons were free.

Since I had missed my first class, I wasn't aware that Britney was at school until I saw her sitting at our usual table in the cafeteria across from Sierra. I wasn't hungry so I bought a bottle of juice before going to sit with them.

"What's up?" I asked as I took my seat.

Britney said, "Tired. I was up late working with Ms. Pearl to get everything ready for Junior's homecoming today."

"Cool. Is your mom coming home today?" Sierra asked.

Britney shook her head up and down. "I wanted to stay home but my dad insisted I come to school."

"We're glad you're back," Sierra said.

I looked around the room. DJ was sitting with his friends at their normal table. He looked at me and smiled. I turned my head away. "Y'all, there's some drama about to go down but you have to promise you won't tell anybody about it."

They pulled their chairs closer together. "Who am I going to tell? You two are the only ones I confide stuff in," Sierra said.

Yeah right. Sierra was bad at keeping a secret. "Last night, when we got back from the hospital, there was an FBI agent at our house."

"Say what?" Britney said.

"My mom and dad found out about the messages some creep left on the message board."

I went on to replay for them the event of the previous night.

"Wow. So they think DJ did it?" Sierra looked in DJ's direction as she talked.

"Girl, I think he did it. It's just too much of a coincidence," I said.

Britney said, "I wouldn't put it past him."

While we were talking, Mr. Reese and Agent Forest and some other man I hadn't seen before walked in the cafeteria. At first I thought they were coming for me, but they walked right past my table to where DJ and his friends were sitting. "That's the agent who was at my house last night," I whispered.

They also turned to look in the same direction. DJ said, "I didn't do anything,"

Mr. Reese said, "Dylan, quiet down. We can handle this in my office."

Everyone in the cafeteria was looking in their direction by now. We watched DJ being escorted out of the cafeteria. I let out a sigh of relief. "I don't know about y'all, but for some reason I'm real thirsty."

DJ would no longer be a thorn in my side, I thought as I drank the rest of my juice. Too bad my parents didn't want the reality TV cameras filming me at school. This would have made a great shot.

35

The Price of Fame

"Do you want to go with me to the hospital?" Britney asked after school as we walked toward her waiting car.

"I can't. My mom will be here any minute," I said. "Hi, Mr. Donovan."

"Ms. Jasmine," he said, as he tilted his head down.

"Call me later," she said as Donovan held her door open.

I waved at them both and waited for my mom to pull up. I was surprised she was late. While waiting on her, my eyes were blinded by a few flashes. The sun was brighter than I thought. I attempted to locate my sunglasses. While I was retrieving them, a man came up with a microphone, "Are you Jasmine McNeil?"

I didn't recognize the man, so I asked, "Who wants to know?"

"I'm a reporter with BT News and you look like her."

I placed my shades on. "There's my mom. I got to go." I avoided his question and ran in the direction I saw my mom driving.

"Girl, you're going to get hit. Get in the car," she yelled as she blocked traffic.

I got in. "Some reporter was trying to ask me questions," I said as I threw my stuff in the backseat and put on my seat belt. I saw a few people taking pictures as we pulled off.

"There are reporters outside of the house too."

"Wow. The show is big news then," I said, trying to figure out how I was going to deal with the fame.

"Someone leaked it to the press that someone was stalking you."

"Mom, I promise I didn't say anything to anybody. Well, Bri and Sierra, but they don't count."

"I know you didn't. It was probably one of the producers on the show."

"Why would they do that? That's crazy."

"Dear, these folks are in it for money. If they can get more attention for their show, they will."

"I can't believe they showed up at my school."

"Neither can I. That's why your dad and I will set up a news conference. Tracking you at school is unacceptable."

I sent Britney and Sierra a text message about the latest drama. We texted each other until we got home. My mom wasn't kidding; there were several news vans on the street outside of our house. Fortunately, our circular driveway was several feet from the curb so they could only take pictures from afar. I saw some of our neighbors being interviewed as we passed by.

We parked behind Brenda's car and rushed into the house. Brenda met us near the door. "The house phone has been ringing off the hook," she said.

"I told you to let the voice mail get it," my mom said as she walked past the living room. "Is your dad back yet?" she asked.

"He's upstairs," Brenda responded.

Once my mom was out of earshot, Brenda said to me, "I didn't want to say anything, but I know who leaked it. It was my now ex-friend Julie."

"I never liked her."

"You don't like any of my friends."

"True." I peeked out the curtain. "This is the most press I've seen since Dad won his last Super Bowl," I said.

Brenda walked up beside me and looked out too.

"I hate losing a friend over this but she's shown me she can't be trusted."

My mom said, "Everybody wants their five minutes of fame."

Brenda turned around. "How much did you hear?"

"Everything."

Brenda held her head down in shame. I left them alone to deal with her ex-friend. I ran into my dad on the way to my room. "Your mom told me about the reporter at school."

"Don't worry. I didn't say anything," I said, trying to reassure him.

"It doesn't matter, because we're about to nip this in the bud now." He hugged me to reassure me all would be okay. "Go change into something nice. Meet me downstairs in thirty minutes."

I didn't know what he had planned but I felt confident that my dad would handle the situation in the best way he knew how. Thirty minutes later, I sat in between him and my mom as Agent Forest went over some of his findings.

"I spoke with Dylan Johnson and he insists he had nothing to do with the messages."

"He's lying," I blurted out.

"Since we're still working our investigation, I had to let him go."

"If he does something to my little girl, I'm going to hold you accountable," my dad said.

"Mr. McNeil, I've been doing this a long time. My gut tells me he's not the one."

"Well, my gut tells me he is," my dad responded.

"I haven't scratched him off our list of suspects, so don't worry about that."

"What about the boy from the Internet?" my mom asked.

"We still haven't been able to locate him." Agent Forest then directed a question at me. "Are you sure you don't have any other information on him?"

I thought about it. I had other e-mails and numbers he had called me from. "Dad, where's the cell bill from last month? He sent me messages and called but I deleted them as soon as I realized they were from him. I can give you the numbers that I don't recognize off the bill," I said.

Less than ten minutes later, my dad walked back in the living room and handed me the cell phone bill. I scanned it and at the agent's persistence, I checked the numbers that didn't look familiar to me. I handed it to him. "These are the numbers I'm not familiar with."

"Jasmine, this is going to help out a lot." Agent Forest scanned the list with some device and made a quick phone call.

There was one good thing about this whole ordeal: my parents were no longer at each other's throat.

"Jasmine, go upstairs and I'll call you down when dinner gets here," my mom said.

"I don't feel like doing homework with all this going on," I said.

"Come on," Brenda said.

Reluctantly, I followed her upstairs to her room. "Did you get in trouble for telling Julie?" I asked.

She put her hands on her hip. "I'm twenty years old. I'm too old to get in trouble."

Yeah right. "Well, Mom didn't look too happy when I left y'all earlier."

"She fussed at me, but that was about it," Brenda said as she retrieved her laptop from its case and we sat on her bed as she logged on.

"I have over a thousand friend requests," Brenda said after she logged on to her MySpace page.

"I want to see what folks are saying about me. Log on to the show's message board," I said.

We scanned some of the messages. A lot of people were upset at the guy going by the name Secret Admirer. If he knew like I knew, he would stay off the boards because some of the comments left for him were violent.

"I never thought being on a show would cause this

many problems," I said as Brenda let me navigate the page.

Brenda responded, "There's a high price to pay for fame."

As much as I enjoyed being the center of attention, I looked forward to the day that everybody would go back to minding their own business.

36

Lights, Cameras, Oops

The reporters were still camped out the next morning when my mom drove me to school. My dad had contacted the media and asked them to not bother me at school. Apparently, there was a law about it, so I would no longer have to worry about flashing cameras when I got dropped off.

DJ and his friends were standing in their usual spot in front of the school, but he turned his back to me when I walked by instead of messing with me like he normally did. Britney and Sierra sat on the bench waiting for me. I didn't bother to sit. "Come on. Let's go inside." I looked around just in case there was a reporter lurking by who didn't follow the rules.

"I can't believe I forgot to put on some lip gloss," I said when we stood in front of the bathroom mirror.

Sierra fluffed her hair. "I'm thinking about cutting it all off."

Britney said, "You go right ahead." She ran her hands through her long brown straight hair. "Scissors better not come close to this."

"Are we still hanging out at your place for our monthly get-together?" I asked Britney.

"Of course." Britney sounded bothered that I asked.

"I was just asking. With your mom just having the babies, I didn't know."

"Precious is breathing on her own now, so she'll be home any day. I hope." Britney appeared to be beaming with pride.

"Your voice changes when you talk about the twins," I commented.

Britney took the lip gloss out of my hand and dabbed some on her lips. "I know I wasn't too happy about them coming . . . but now that they're here I love them."

The bell rang so our bathroom session ended. As we were talking and walking out the bathroom, we ran smack into DJ and his friends. "Hey, watch it," Britney said.

"Excuse me," DJ said. "Jasmine, can I talk to you for a minute?"

Sierra walked and stood in front of me. "We don't think that's a good idea."

I placed my arm on her shoulder. "Let him say what he has to say."

Sierra crossed her arms. "Fine, but we're not going anywhere."

DJ said to his friends, "I'll catch up with y'all later."

"I'm sorry about the things I said about you," he said, attempting to sound apologetic.

I laughed and snapped my fingers a few times. "Apology not accepted."

"I told that cop that I didn't write those things on that board," he tried to assure me.

"But you did write that stuff on MySpace and according to my dad, that's a federal offense." I crossed my arms.

Sierra calmly said, "I bet you won't be harassing anybody else. Now, will you?"

DJ sneered. "This isn't about you."

Annoyed, I said, "Look, you wanted to talk to me." I looked at Sierra and then at Britney. "You either talk to all or talk to none."

"Fine. I admit to the MySpace thing but I swear I didn't leave any messages on the message board. I wouldn't do something like that."

"La-la-la. There's a liar in our midst," Britney hummed.

"And his name is Dylan Johnson," I added.

Dylan turned beet-red. "No wonder the guy is harassing you. You act like a b—"

"Mr. Johnson, I know you're not about to call this young lady outside of her name," Ms. Houston said as she walked up to us.

"No, ma'am," he said, lowering his voice as he walked off.

"Ladies, you need to be getting to class."

"Yes, ma'am," we all said as we headed to our homeroom class.

Later, during study period, Cecil was unusually quiet. "I think you need to find another tutor." He sounded like he lost his best friend.

"I don't want another tutor. I want you." I hoped he could read in between the lines.

"I saw the preview of next week's show," he sadly said.

Oh man. Maybe I shouldn't have said anything about him on camera. "Cecil, I was just saying that around my girls. You know. Girl talk."

"What you said is going to be shown to millions of people. Don't you know everybody in the school is watching it because you're on there?"

I smiled. This would help me make the cheerleaders squad. Popularity was real important when it came to being a cheerleader.

"Jasmine," Cecil said my name a few times. I could see the sadness in his eyes.

"Sorry, my mind sort of wandered. Where was I? Nobody is going to care. I don't think I ever said your name." I couldn't remember if I did, but I couldn't lose Cecil as my tutor or my friend. I liked him more than I cared to admit to him or my friends.

Cecil gathered up his books. Sounding upset, he said, "Find yourself another tutor."

"Cecil," I begged as some of the other students looked on.

Cecil ignored me and left the study room. What was I going to do? I had a test coming up. I threw my stuff in my backpack and rushed out the room to find him. I ran until I caught up with him and reached for his arm. "Cecil, wait. Let me explain."

"Get yourself another—what's the word you used—yes, 'nerd on steroids,' because I'm no longer available," he said in a trembling voice.

He kept walking. I had to run in order to keep up with him. I ran in front of him. He moved to one side. I moved right in front of him. We played the walk-and-move game until he gave up. "Listen, Cecil. I apologize, okay. Yes, I was wrong for saying what I said, but I only did that because I didn't want my friends to know I liked you."

"You what?" He finally stopped trying to move.

I grabbed his hand. "I like you. I know it came out of nowhere. Who would think someone who looks like me would want a guy like you, but I do." That didn't quite come out right, but hopefully he got the point.

Cecil started stammering, "I never thought—you always blow me off."

"Silly, that's because I didn't even know I liked you."

Cecil started to move. "Oh, I see. You're just saying this so I can help you pass your test. I'm not falling for that trick."

"I'm not playing. I'm serious. If you don't believe me, ask Sierra. Ask Britney."

Cecil looked at me like he doubted me. I had to think of something quick. I really did like him and I needed him not only to pass my test, but I liked hanging out with him too.

"I don't believe you, but I thought about it. It would be wrong for me to leave you hanging right before a test."

I hugged him. My head came to his chest. "You're the best. You won't regret it." I grabbed his hand and led him back to the study area. Other students were looking at us, but I ignored the stares.

I pulled out my book and notebook. "I need to know why X doesn't equal Z and why."

I snuggled up closer to him as he wrote down the steps I would need to solve the problem. He didn't have to say it, because his actions showed me that he had forgiven me.

37

More Drama More Problems

"You got my cousin arrested." Marcus confronted me while we were standing around Britney's locker the next morning.

I said, "Marcus, I don't know what you're talking about." I turned back around to talk to Britney and Sierra.

"He didn't do it and you know it."

Britney moved to stand in front of Marcus. "I don't know why you're taking up for him, but since you are, you need to get out of my face."

I could always depend on my girls having my back.

"I know he didn't do it and it's wrong for you to accuse him."

"Bri, move. I got this." I turned around and made sure Marcus could read my facial expressions. "DJ, your cousin, has been harassing me this entire semester. If you think for one moment that I am feeling sorry for him, think again. He shouldn't have done it."

Sierra added, "He's exactly where he should be."

We gave each other high fives. Marcus said to Britney. "I can't believe you are this heartless. To think I still wanted to be with you."

"Well, Marcus, news flash. I don't want you and hadn't wanted you since last year."

"Bu-yah . . . now, will you move because we have to get to class," I said as I used my hand to push him.

While we were walking away Britney said, "He got his nerves. I'm so through with Marcus."

"Looks like Travis is all the way in the house," I said as Sierra and I tapped each other on the hand.

The whole homeroom class was buzzing, but when we entered the room, they all got quiet.

"Is it true DJ sent you those messages?" one girl asked me.

"He told me you probably left yourself those messages," this guy said.

Sierra said, "Really. Did he also tell you he's been harassing her all semester? I'm sure he didn't have to because you could see for yourself."

"Class, you all need to be seated," Mrs. Johnson said when she walked in the room.

I turned around in my seat. I can't recall what Mrs. Johnson lectured on because my mind was on DJ's arrest. My nightmare was finally over.

Later that afternoon, instead of doing homework, I surfed the Internet and read about DJ's arrest. Since he was a minor, they never mentioned his name in the articles, but I knew they were talking about him. They did mention it was a Plano High student. I disregarded my homework. Who could think with all of this going on? Britney called to give me an update on the twins. I told her about the media camped out in front of our house. Sierra called on my other end. "They're talking about you on channel eight," she said.

"Bri, turn your TV on channel eight. Hold on."

I clicked back over to Sierra. "Hang up and I'll call you right back." Between turning on the TV and getting Sierra back on the phone, I missed the first part, but tuned in just in time to see my parents standing outside of our house. Lily was standing next to them. My father said, "We would like to take the time to thank the show's producers for handling this matter expediently." He looked in Lily's direction. She smiled. "We would also hope that the media would respect our fourteen-year-old daughter's privacy. We understand that this is newsworthy but we do not want to subject her to any more heartache if we can."

One of the reporters in the audience asked, "Why did you agree to have her filmed with you on the show if you didn't want her in the spotlight?"

"At the time, we weren't anticipating someone harassing her. If I would have suspected that, believe me, I never would have agreed to it," he responded.

"What are your plans now? Will the show air the remainder of the episodes?" a female reporter asked.

Lily stepped in front of the microphone. "Yes, we have discussed this with the McNeils. The rest of the shows will air as scheduled."

"Do you think being on the show has helped you and your wife patch up your differences?"

My dad and mom looked at each other. He responded, "I would prefer not to answer that at this time. Kim and I have a lot to work out."

Lily tried to lighten up the situation. She added, "You have to watch the show to find out the answer to that."

"Is the boy they have in custody the one who's been harassing your daughter?"

"I don't know the answers to that right now. All I can tell you is that it's still under investigation."

Another question came from the audience. "Isn't it true you only did the show to get the sports-commentator position because you need the money since you had to close a few dealerships?"

My dad placed his arm around my mom and led her away from the podium. I watched them as the camera followed them back into the house. The news commentator said, "Stay tuned for further updates on this situation. Viewers, text your answer to today's question. Do you monitor your teen's Internet usage? Your responses will be aired at ten o'clock."

I clicked off the television. "Wow, your dad sure knows how to handle them," Britney said.

"Don't say anything because I know you won't believe this, but I regret filling out that application now," I said. If I couldn't admit my mistakes to my friends, then who could I admit them to?

Sierra was the first to speak. "Your parents seem like they're doing okay."

"But for how long?"

Britney said, "Things could work out. All of this may have happened for a reason."

"I hope so. I got to call y'all back. I hear my mama calling me," I said as I hung up with them.

"I saw y'all on TV," I said to my parents when I located them in the dining room.

"I missed it," Brenda said as she piled some food on her plate.

"Well, let's hope the boy they have in custody is the right one," my mom said as she placed a glass of ice in front of each of us.

"From what I read on the Net, he was an all-star varsity player. He's going to lose a lot," Brenda said.

"Being a jock doesn't excuse his behavior," my dad said, right before saying prayer.

After the prayer, we were all in our own little worlds as we ate. It was good not to have the *Situation Number Nine* people around any more. Being in the spotlight wasn't all I thought it would be. In fact, it brought more drama and more problems.

38

New Attitude

"**I** can't stay on the phone with you all night." I giggled after one of Cecil's comments. He quizzed me over the phone to help prepare me for my test and two hours later, we were still on the phone. I no longer found his corny jokes corny.

My phone beeped. I thought it was one of my girls so I didn't bother to look at the caller ID when I told Cecil to hold on. "You got the wrong guy," someone whispered from the other end. The call disconnected. I pulled the phone away from my ear. *Unknown* showed on the display. I clicked back over to Cecil. "Somebody's playing on the phone."

"Probably one of DJ's friends," Cecil said.

"Or Marcus." I told him about Marcus's confrontation earlier.

"After what he did to Marcus, I'm surprised," Cecil said.

"Family takes up for family," I said. Unless they're my family. My cousins were haters.

"If anyone messes with you again, let me know."

"Aw, that's so sweet," I said, teasing him.

"I know you're not my girl but I do like you. And maybe after I finish tutoring you, we can go out sometime."

"Maybe so," I said. I felt butterflies in my stomach.

I hung up with Cecil and went to bed.

The next day, when I got to school, I ran right into DJ. "What are you doing here?" I asked.

"Trying to get an education just like you," he snapped and walked away.

I ran behind him. "I thought you were in jail."

"I can't talk to you."

"Oh, now you don't want to talk." I dialed my mom's number. "DJ's at school."

I heard her yell, "Dion. Your dad's coming up to the school right now. Don't go anywhere near him. You hear me, Jasmine."

Too late. "Yes, ma'am."

Sierra ran up to me. "I think I should warn you. DJ's here."

"I saw him."

As Sierra and I walked to homeroom, students and teachers watched us as we walked down the hallway. The tension in the air was thick. I took my seat at the front of the class and tuned out the noise around me. I tapped my foot as I waited for Mrs. Johnson to come in the class. To my disappointment, Mr. White, the substitute teacher that I didn't like, appeared.

"Hi, all. By now you all know I'm Mr. White. Mrs. Johnson will be out today and she's asked me to give you a pop quiz since she couldn't be here."

We all moaned. I rushed behind Sierra when class was over. "Girl, he still gives me the creeps," I said.

"He was watching you the whole time," Britney stated.

"I didn't even look his way. I'm glad he didn't ask me to stay after class this time or else I was going to have to report him. I've had my fill of perverts."

Britney answered her vibrating cell phone. "That's my mom. Precious got a good doctor's report."

"You're really into this baby stuff, aren't you?" I asked.

"I try to help my mama feed them, although having a nanny sure does help. Precious doesn't cry much but Junior—oh my goodness. He cries too much."

I listened to Britney talk about her little sister and brother until we reached the end of the hallway; afterward we parted and went our separate ways. My phone vibrated before I could make it to class. It was my dad's number. "Hi, Dad."

"Meet me at Mr. Reese's office," he said.

I did as I was told. Upon reaching the office, Mr. Reese, my dad, DJ, and DJ's dad were seated around the desk. I took a seat next to my dad. Mr. Reese said, "Now that all parties are here, I wanted to see if we could work something out that we can all agree on."

My dad said, "I want him expelled from school. That's the only thing I will agree to."

Mr. Johnson said, "If memory serves me correctly, your daughter was all over my son the first time I met her."

He was talking about the party at Marcus's. I remembered back in the fall going with Britney and her folks. That was when I thought I liked DJ. That was before I found out he was a jerk. I shifted in my seat. I couldn't deny it because he was telling the truth about that, so I said, "DJ knows I don't like him like that. Since then, he's made it a point to say mean stuff about me . . . about my friends."

Mr. Reese looked at Mr. Johnson. "Unfortunately, we have several girls who can vouch for DJ's behavior."

"And he's still here. I'm suing the school and the whole Plano school district," my dad said.

"Mr. McNeil, there's no need for that."

"You just admitted to knowingly subjecting my daughter and no telling how many other young girls to the likes of him." He pointed at DJ.

"Son, is there anything you would like to say," Mr. Johnson said, in a calm voice.

DJ barely looked up. "Jasmine, I would like to apologize for my behavior. I promise to never say a bad thing about you again."

"He can keep that sorry apology. Mr. Reese, you will be hearing from my attorney. Jasmine, get your stuff, we're leaving."

My dad stood up and I followed behind him. "Dad, I like this school. Please let me stay. I don't have to see DJ. If I see him coming, I'll walk the other way."

I couldn't believe I said I liked Plano High. At the beginning of the school year, I didn't want to be here; now I had a new attitude about the school. My friends were here. Cecil was here.

He stopped abruptly. "I'll think about it. But you're going home for the rest of the day until I can figure some things out."

My mom wasn't too happy about him pulling me out of school and they argued for the first time in a long time. I put the earplugs to my iPod in my ear to drown out the noise. I sent Britney and Sierra a text message to their cell phones. I hoped they looked at it before lunchtime. There wasn't anything on TV that caught my attention, so I listened to my music and took a nap.

The phone vibrating by my ear woke me up. It was Cecil checking on me. I sent him a quick text to let him know that all was well. "No wonder my stomach is growling," I said, after glancing at the clock.

I rushed down the stairs to see what leftovers I could find in the refrigerator. I ended up making a sandwich. I sure missed having a cook. Fortunately for me, my mom still made me do things myself or I would be helpless.

39

Oh No

I didn't go to school for the rest of the week. I spent most of the time in my room reading books. I had just stopped reading to play a video game when my mom summoned me downstairs. I thought dinner was ready because everybody was in the dining room. I wasn't expecting to see Agent Forest.

"Brenda, we need to talk to Jasmine alone," my mom said.

Brenda looked at me to see if I knew why. I shrugged my shoulders. I stood just in case I needed to make a quick exit.

My mom walked up to me and grabbed my arm and escorted me to the table. From the looks on my parents' faces, things didn't look good. Agent Forest didn't waste any time. "We thought we had the right person, but it looks like Dylan Johnson is not our guy."

"He has to be," I yelled.

"My team was able to track down the guy you met on the Internet by tracing his IP address."

"Are you sure the guy didn't do anything to you? Did he touch you in any way that was inappropriate?"

"No, Mom. I told y'all. I never really met him. It was just that one time at the mall."

"Agent Forest just informed us the guy you've been communicating with is in his twenties. He's not seventeen as you thought," my dad said.

"What? But the picture he sent me . . . he looked seventeen." I turned to face my mom. "If you would have seen him in person, you would have thought he was seventeen too."

My memory went back to the short encounter at the mall. I really didn't get a good look at him because the bus windows were tinted. While I was trying to reenact our encounter in my mind, my dad handed me a picture. "This is the picture of Talland-Fly," he said.

I did a double take. "This can't be. This is Mr. White," I said.

"Who is Mr. White?" my mom asked.

"He substitutes at my school. He substituted for Mrs. Johnson's class this morning."

"What kind of people do they have teaching my child?" my dad asked. "I'm pulling you out of Plano immediately."

I thought about it for a moment. If I went to another school, I wouldn't get to see my friends as much. "No, Dad, don't do that."

"You can't go back to that school with perverts like him running around," my mom said.

"Kim, go find me the principal's number. This is the last straw."

"Calm down, Mr. and Mrs. McNeil," Agent Forest said. "Let me update my team on this new information. William White will regret he ever crossed our paths." He dialed someone on the phone.

I got up to go find Brenda. "Where are you going, young lady? Get back here," my mom said.

"I'll be right back. Promise." Brenda was in the living room. "Bren, your classmate is TallandFly."

I told her what Agent Forest had told me. "I can't believe it. He was all in my face. I could kick his butt myself. There was always something weird about that guy."

"I can't believe it. All this time Mr. White has been the one I've been talking to on the Net."

"This is crazy. I hope they catch the nut."

I called Britney and Sierra to tell them the news. Sierra was shocked. "You kept saying there was something strange about him."

"But he didn't look like the picture you showed us," Britney said.

"It must have been an old picture." I couldn't believe I almost became a victim.

Sierra added, "And he told us his name was Billy White."

Britney concluded, "Billy could be short for William."

By now, I was standing in the dining room doorway. "I'll call y'all back when I find out more."

Agent Forest reassured my parents. "Dallas PD is on the way with some of our men to pick him up now."

"What's the address? I'll meet them there." My dad stood up. I could tell he was nervous from the tone of his voice.

Agent Forest didn't budge. In an authoritative voice, he said, "It's best if you wait here with me."

Upset, my dad responded, "I have to protect my girl. I want to make sure they get the guy."

"With my agents and DPD working together, he's as good as ours. The best thing you can do is wait right here. Sit. Talk and be here with your family."

My dad didn't sit. Instead, I watched him pace the floor.

My mom and I took turns playing UNO on my BlackBerry. Brenda called around to see if anyone else knew more on William, Billy, or whatever name he was going by.

"Dion, you need to sit down. You're making me nervous," my mom said, as I beat her in another hand of UNO.

At that moment, Agent Forest's phone rang. We all looked in his direction. It was hard to read his facial expression. "They got him."

"Yes!" I excitedly said.

"What do I need to do . . . any papers I need to fill out? Just tell me so I can make sure he doesn't get out to solicit another young girl," my dad said.

"Unfortunately for him, it'll be awhile before he gets out. When they busted him, they confiscated some things that will keep him locked up for some time," Agent Forest said. He turned and looked at me. "Young lady, you were lucky this time. I want you to promise me, and your parents, that you will not be trying to meet up with anyone you meet on the Internet anymore."

After all this drama, that was the last thing they had to worry about. "I've learned my lesson," I said as my mom wrapped her arms around me.

40

Growing Up

It didn't take long for the media to swarm outside of our house. "Y'all don't have to talk to them if you don't want to," Agent Forest said.

"I'll do it. There's something I want to say," I responded.

"Oh, no, young lady, your time in the limelight is over," my mom said in a protective tone.

"Mom, please. I have to do this. I need to in order to put this behind me."

My dad looked at me and hesitantly said, "Fine. Agent Forest, tell them we'll be out to talk to them in a few minutes but on one condition. There will not be a question-and-answer session."

Agent Forest followed his instructions. "Brenda,

you don't have to go out there if you don't want to," my dad said.

In typical Brenda fashion, she asked, "We're still a family, aren't we?" My dad nodded his head. "So, let's go do this," she said.

My mom made sure we all looked presentable. Brenda and I followed behind our parents into the front lawn. My dad cleared his throat. "We want to thank the media for helping expose guys like William White. I want to publicly apologize to the young man who got falsely accused. He's guilty of some things, but not this crime. We hope that this will straighten him up."

My mom took over for him at this point. My normally cool mother seemed a little shaky as she stepped up to the microphone. "Against my better judgment, my daughter has something she wants to say about all of this. Dear."

Now that the microphones and cameras were all on me, I wasn't so sure if I could talk. My heart was beating so fast, I just knew others could hear it. I closed my eyes for a few seconds and then opened them up and said what came from the heart. "I learned a valuable lesson about using the Internet. My friends . . . people at school . . . we all hear about the dangers of talking to strangers on the Internet . . .

but to be honest . . . I never thought something like this could happen to me. I always said . . . I would know if the person on the other end of the computer was a pervert . . . I didn't think the person would lie about their age . . . or send me an old picture . . . if my friends hadn't gone with me that day . . . who knows what would have happened to me." My mom squeezed my hand. I was glad she did, because I didn't know if I could finish what I wanted to say. When I saw the pride in her eyes and in my dad's eyes, I continued. "I'm lucky—correction—blessed . . . that God watched over me because all of this could have turned out differently. I want other girls to be safe and the only way to be safe is to not talk to strangers on the Internet. Thank you."

Everyone there clapped. My dad, sounding all choked up, said, "That'll be all." We all left and went back into the house.

Agent Forest said, "Young lady, what you did will help some other young lady. Even little boys have to be careful. Predators don't discriminate as long as they can manipulate a young mind."

My dad extended his hand out to Agent Forest. "Thanks for finding the man."

"I'm glad it worked out the way it did," he responded, and made his exit.

"Half-pint, you gave me a few more gray hairs." My dad wrapped his arms around me. I felt safe in his arms.

"Dad, you don't have any hair."

"It's growing underneath." We laughed.

Before going to bed I called Britney and Sierra. "Did y'all watch the news?"

"Yes, my mom said you sounded very mature," Britney said as she imitated her mother's voice.

"I meant what I said. We need to make a pact right now that none of us will ever *ever* meet a guy off the Internet like that again."

"I promise." Britney was the first to speak.

"I pinky swear promise," Sierra said.

"I have one more phone call to make and then I can go to bed." I was feeling a little more upbeat now that I was talking to my two BFFs.

Britney sang, "Jasmine has a boyfriend."

"Not yet, now bye." I hit the end button on my phone and scrolled through my address book and clicked on Cecil's name. He didn't answer. I was about to leave him a message when he called me back on my other line. "For a minute, I thought you didn't want to talk to me." I pretended to pout.

"Jas, I saw the news. I would have called but I didn't know if you felt like talking."

"I'll always have time for you, CC."

"You sound like my little sister. I hate when she calls me that."

"Do I look like your little sister?"

"Well, y'all are about the same height," he teased.

"Oh, you got jokes. I might be short, but ask DJ, I can sure hit hard."

"Speaking of DJ, one of my friends told me they heard he might be transferring schools."

"Since it wasn't him, he won't have to."

"Rumor has it your dad threatened to sue the school, so Mr. Reese was setting it up."

"My dad did say he was going to sue . . . to be honest, I hope DJ does transfer."

"Me . . . you . . . and all the other people he's tried to bully."

I fell asleep on the phone with Cecil.

"Jasmine Charlotte, I've told you about that phone," my mom angrily said the next morning.

"Today's Saturday, so why are you waking me up so early?" I asked.

"Don't be getting sassy with me. I can wake you up whenever I want to. This is my house and until you get grown—I pulled the covers back over my head, as she went on a rant.

"Get up. We have a spa day and then afterward we're going to the Galleria."

I threw the covers back. Excited, I responded, "Really. Give me thirty minutes. Well, forty minutes and I'll be ready." She knew exactly what to say to get me out of bed.

41

Behind Closed Doors

Brenda didn't go to the spa with us. It was just my mom and I. I got the works. I got my ends clipped on my hair. After a little pleading and begging, my mom let me get some highlights. While waiting on the beautician to finish her hair, I primped in the mirror. It was hard to decide on which flavor of lip gloss to wear. I was in a good mood, so I chose very berry.

"Girl, you need to stay out the mirror," my mom said as she walked by.

I followed her. "I like your hair like that," I said.

"It does make me look younger, doesn't it?"

"I didn't say all that, Mom." She popped me on the arm. It actually did make her look younger. She could pass for my older sister.

After eating a light lunch, we headed to the Galleria. We were waiting to check out, when someone behind us said, "That is them. That's the people from that show *Situation Number Nine.*"

I turned around to see a group of women who looked twice as old as my mom on her bad day. I was ready to move on to the next store, but after they all wanted our autographs, my mom was more than happy to oblige. Thirty minutes later, we were headed to Saks. My mom said, "I thought we would never get out of there."

"You should have just told them no and we could have been out of there sooner," I said, hauling the bags as my mom's hands remained empty except for the purse strap around her fingers.

"Dear, you'll learn that you never know when you'll need someone, so it's always best to treat everybody the way you want to be treated."

"But we're shopping. They need to respect our privacy."

"Remember that when you see your favorite celebrity out and about," she said.

"I am so not like those people." I rolled my eyes.

"If Soulja Boy were to walk in this mall today, would you go up to him?" she asked with a huge smile on her face.

"Of course. He would remember me anyway. I have one of those faces." I smiled, showing all of my teeth.

"You are your father's child," my mom responded as we continued our walk to Saks.

"I think this will be our last stop because Saks is having a sale," my mom said with some excitement in her voice.

There was a huge sign with *40 percent off* displayed across it. I picked up my pace and we went from department to department. We did so much shopping that my mom decided to have the stuff delivered to the house instead of us having to carry it all back to the car. I was in the dressing room trying on clothes, when I heard someone on the other side of the door say, "His wife thinks she's all that. If he knew she was in here spending all of his money, he would have a fit."

Another woman spoke. "So what are you going to do?"

"I'm calling Dion now. That heifer is spending up money he could be putting in my pocket."

I couldn't believe my ears. Was this woman talking about my daddy? They continued to talk. I sent Britney and Sierra text messages. They advised me to stay in the dressing room, when all I wanted to do was go out and find out for sure who they were talking about.

The other woman said, "Shhh . . . here she comes."

"Quick, stand in front of me. I don't want her to see me," the other woman said.

I tried to jump up so I could see her face but couldn't. I opened the door slightly and got a glimpse of a red shirt and blue jeans on one lady and a pink shirt and blue jeans on another. I didn't know who was who. My mom called out my name, "Jasmine, you ready. I told Dion I would cook tonight but I need to make a run to the grocery store first."

I knew then the woman's Dion was my dad. I flung open the door. The women eased their way out of the dressing area without my mom noticing them. "Mom, there's something I need to tell you."

Her phone rang. I paced the floor as I waited for her. Should I keep it to myself? Her and my dad seemed so happy. What if the Dion the woman was talking about was somebody else's man and not my dad?

"Jasmine, now what did you have to tell me?" she asked after ending her phone call.

"Nothing," I lied.

I flew out the dressing room at that point, hoping to at least put a face to the voices I just heard. "Slow down girl," my mom said, walking behind me. "You act like the devil is after you."

The devil wasn't after me but she was sure after my daddy.

I got a brief look at both women as they turned around just when they were exiting the store. I recalled seeing that same woman in the picture with my dad on the gossip blog. My dad had a lot of explaining to do.

It seemed like it took us forever to go to the grocery store and then get home. Britney and Sierra kept sending me text messages telling me I needed to mind my own business. My parents were my business.

My dad was upstairs when we arrived home. "Mom, I'll take your bags up to your room for you."

"Thanks. I'll go ahead and get dinner started. Tell your dad to come downstairs when he gets a chance."

I kissed her on the cheek and went upstairs. I didn't bother to knock on their bedroom door. He looked guilty as he threw his phone on the bed. "Did y'all buy the whole store?" he asked.

"I'm pretty sure your girlfriend has already given you the four-one-one," I snapped.

"Young lady, you better watch your mouth."

I placed the bags down on the chaise and went to

confront him. "You better be glad Mama didn't hear your girlfriend."

"Listen, little girl. I have no idea what you're talking about."

"You're supposed to be setting an example. How am I ever supposed to trust guys when my own daddy lies to me?" I stormed out their room and went to my room.

My dad was on my heels so I couldn't slam the door like I wanted to. He closed the door. "Jasmine, have a seat."

I crossed my arms and didn't move. "You promised me you would try. You did the show . . . the counseling . . . why, Daddy . . . why?" I asked as tears flowed down my cheeks.

"Your mama makes me feel insecure. Cheryl . . . she makes me feel wanted . . . needed," he responded.

I picked up a pillow off my bed and threw it at him. "I need you . . . isn't that enough?" I slid on top of the covers and wouldn't stop crying.

He rushed by my side and tried to console me. My mother walked in the room. "I can hear y'all downstairs. Jasmine, what's going on? Is that William guy trying to call you from jail?"

I turned and faced my mom. No words would come out of my mouth. Instead, I turned away and cried into my pillow.

"Dion, you better tell me what's wrong with my baby."

"Kim, come on. Let's take this conversation elsewhere."

"No. You're going to talk to me right here and now."

I felt my dad sit on the edge of my bed. I turned my head to see my mom walk closer toward him.

"Baby, I tried . . . but this . . . this isn't working out."

I had never seen my mom look like she did at that moment when he said that. Barely above a whisper, she said, "What's not working out?"

He moved one of his hands and pointed at himself and then at her. "This . . . you . . . me . . . us. I tried, but baby . . . I still want a divorce."

My mom walked a few more steps and slapped him. My dad's hand flew up to his face. I shot up in bed. "Don't you call me *baby* ever again. I want you out now. Out of my house . . . out of my life."

She stormed away. My dad looked at me for comfort, but I didn't have any words for him. At this point, I was on my mom's side. I was ready for him to get ghost and leave us. "I love you, half-pint," he said. He paused, hoping for a response from me, but I didn't give him one. He leaned down and kissed me on the forehead and left.

A part of my heart left with him. All I had now were memories. After all I had done to keep them together my parents were still getting a divorce. To release some of my frustrations, I threw my pillows on the floor and then laid back on my bed and cried.

42

Splitsville

Several weeks had passed since my parents' fight in my room. My dad was staying at a corporate apartment not far from us. He had been asking me to dinner since he left, but I didn't want to cause my mom any more grief, so I would tell him I didn't want to. I wanted him to feel the pain we felt. Even Brenda walked around like she was depressed and she was the main one telling me our parents should divorce.

My mom eventually gave me permission to spend time with my dad. I didn't want her to know it but I felt relieved. I missed him. When he called to let me know he was right around the corner, I decided to wait for him outside of the house so my mom wouldn't have to see him.

"Get in, half-pint," he said when he pulled up.

I would have to talk to him about his little nickname. I was no longer a child, so that name would have to go. "Hey, Dad." I hopped in his SUV and buckled up my seat belt.

"So where do you want to eat?" he asked as he pulled away.

"It doesn't matter," I responded. It felt awkward. He tried to make small talk with me, but it only made the situation worse.

"Your mom told me you were trying out for cheerleaders."

When did they talk? The last time I heard my mom talking about him, she was taking him to the cleaners.

"Yeah. If I get chosen, I'll need some money to go to cheerleading camp."

"It'll be taken care of. Don't worry yourself about that."

I decided on Chinese food so he took me to our favorite Chinese restaurant. He did manage to get a few laughs out of me. The conversation during the drive home wasn't as awkward as before.

"Have you had any more problems at school?" he asked.

"Not since DJ left," I responded.

"Good. If anybody messes with you again . . . you let me know. I'll take care of it."

When we pulled up in front of the house, I said, "Thanks, Dad, for dinner."

"Can we do this again next week?"

I smiled and paused. "Next week is my week to host the sleepover."

"Oh yeah, I forgot. I know better than to interrupt that. Maybe Sunday after church, then."

I leaned over and kissed him on the cheek. "Maybe."

He smiled and waited for me to get in the house.

My mom sat at the bottom of the stairway. "Did you have a good time with your father?"

"Yes, ma'am." I went and sat by her and draped my arms around her. "Thanks for letting me go."

"Contrary to what's going on between us, he's still your dad. I don't want to keep you away from each other."

"I still think he's a jerk for leaving."

"I kicked him out, remember."

"Well, if he didn't do what he did you wouldn't have had to kick him out," I said.

"You remember when I said you're your daddy's girl . . . I was wrong . . . you're just like me and don't you ever change."

My mom hugged me tight and we sat that way for a few minutes before I went upstairs.

The following Friday, Britney, Sierra and I were in my room in our pajamas surfing the Internet and looking at the gossip blogs. Sierra tried to click off one of the gossip pages before I could see it, but it was too late. The blog header read *SPLITSVILLE for Situation Number Nine Couple.*

"They need to mind their own business," I said as I turned the laptop around so I could get a clearer view of the blog post.

I read it out loud: "According to our sources, Kim has gotten tired of Dion and kicked him out of the house for cheating with the maid. This *Situation Number Nine* Couple is the first couple who didn't come out reconciled. I wonder what will happen to Jasmine, who is rumored to be getting her own reality show soon. Be sure to stop back by here for the latest and greatest in entertainment news."

"Do y'all see this? No wonder my mom said you can't believe everything you read online, because the only thing true about that whole post is that my mama kicked him out."

Sierra said, "You said he did cheat."

I rolled my eyes at her. "It wasn't with a maid . . . and when did I get my own show."

Britney interrupted us. "I think it's time to turn the computer off."

"Please do," I said as I pushed the laptop back in front of Sierra.

My cell phone rang. It was Cecil. I talked to him for

a few minutes before ending the call. A few minutes later, Britney got a phone call from Travis. "Am I the only one who doesn't have a boyfriend?" Sierra asked.

"We don't have boyfriends," Britney said.

I sang, "We just some playa playas."

"And you know it," Britney said, giving me a high five.

"Y'all are silly," Sierra said.

I reached behind my bed and handed them each a square box with a ribbon on it. "These came today."

I watched the smiles come over their faces as they each opened up the container filled with a variety of lip gloss with their personalized names written on the tubes. "Thank you, Jas." Britney got up and hugged me. Sierra did the same.

"I shop when I'm depressed. With all the drama between my parents . . . I did a lot of shopping."

Britney, forever the voice of reason, said, "My mom said when parents divorce, they are divorcing each other, not you."

Sierra tried to lighten the mood. She said, "Something good did come from all of this."

"Name one," I said.

"DJ's no longer at Plano High."

We each held up a tube of lip gloss and did an air

toast. "Hip-hip hooray." A celebration was truly in order. Not only was I celebrating DJ's departure, but my friends. My parents divorcing would be an adjustment, but at least I had my friends to help me deal with it.

ACKNOWLEDGMENTS

Without God in my life, none of this would be possible. I thank him for allowing me to live my dreams.

To my readers: I hope the topics in my books not only entertain you, but encourage you long after you've read the last page.

Special thanks to:

Exie Goss—my mom and number-one supporter. Due to her encouragement as a child, I have grown up knowing that I could be anything I wanted to be with hard work and faith. Thank you Mom and Dad (Lloyd Goss: 1947–1996).

Kaelen Barclay (Carla's daughter), Angelia Menchan, Dr. Sharon Gray and her Georgia high school students—I appreciate you reading *The Lip Gloss Chronicles* during its early stages and providing feedback.

Maxine Thompson, my agent, and Carl Weber, my publisher—thank you both for believing in this project.

Martha, Natalie, Brenda, Kevin, and the rest of the

Urban Books and Kensington Books family—thank you for adding your magic touch.

Kandie Delley of KanDel Media—thank you for the wonderful job you did on the *Lip Gloss Chronicles* Web site (www.thelipglosschronicles.com).

To the librarians, teachers, book clubs, Webmasters, and readers—thank you. I appreciate you all for reading and sharing the news of *The Lip Gloss Chronicles*. I would like to thank the Shreve Memorial Library for reaching out to me before the books were published.

Last, but not least, I want to dedicate this book to John, DeAngelo, Cameron, Justin, Jerricka (my little diva), Jasmine (my best little friend), Ellen (mini-me), and Markessia (my LGC model). You are our future. I pray that God guide and protect you during your childhood years. Know that your auntie and/or older cousin loves you all. If you can dream it, you can be it.

Shelia M. Goss

ABOUT THE AUTHOR

Shelia M. Goss is the national bestselling author of *The Ultimate Test*, the first book in the *Lip Gloss Chronicles* series. Besides writing books for teens, she writes women's fiction. She's garnered awards and accolades since writing fiction. Be sure to stop by *Lip Gloss Chronicles* Web site (www.thelipglosschronicles. com) and sign up for updates on contests, free excerpts, and more.